Story Time With Crazy Uncle Matt

a tangle of yarns
by
Matt Spencer

Back Roads Carnival Books,
Brattleboro, Vermont

BACK ROADS CARNIVAL BOOKS
mattspencerauthor.wordpress.com

ISBN: 978-0-692-15638-4

OTHER BOOKS BY MATT SPENCER

The Night and the Land
The Trail of the Beast
Cult of the Stars
Chapel of the Falcon
Summer Reaping on the Fields of Nowhere
Shadow Ballads
The Drifting Soul

For Laura

Some folks I'd like to thank personally for their love, support, friendship, and inspiration over the years, in relation to this volume and the stories herein...and/or for other reasons some of them probably wouldn't want me to talk about publicly: Kurt Amacker, Ian Bigelow, Luke Burke, Garrett Cook, Jay Craven, Cyndal Ellis, Amanda Fish, Matthew Gomez, Bill Hilburn, Jack Holder, Sydney Isle, Laura Janisieski, Emyli McGrath, Alyse Landis, Kay Lemay, Julian McTaggart, Cameron Mount, Lucia Morey, Luz Elena Morey, Paul Peterson, Peggy Peterson, Mitchel Quelch, Aaron Ryan, Dan Seitz, Stephen Seitz, Michael Waggoner, Joy Walker, Sheryl Westleigh, and Shayna Williams.

In loving memory: Aaron Rodenbaugh, Mike Dabney, David Pierce, Kareem Hairston

Author's Note

These stories span a ten-year period of my career as a professional storyteller, of my life as an ever-evolving person. Some of them were previously included in my first collection, *Shadow Ballads*. So to all ten of you who already have a copy of that little volume, sorry for the double-dip. While preparing this collection, I gave each of these stories a fresh spit an' polish, ran them by some new, better editors, but resisted the urge to significantly re-write any of them. The older pieces are the feverish creations of a younger man, and it would feel wrong to impose the sensibilities of this cranky old bastard on what that spitfire kid had to say. I'm not George Lucas. Cassias totally stabbed first. I chose all these stories because I still like them, in some cases love them, and/or because they were especially well received upon their original publication. They're not presented in any order so far as writing or publication dates. Rather, I fell back on my old radio DJ instincts, presenting the stories as a fluctuation of moods, themes, styles, and attitudes, like a good, hard-rockin' song mix.

Welcome to the carnival, folks. Don't get lost, unless that's what you came here to do.

Contents

The Room Above The Bar
on River Street

How enough people ever found that dump to keep it in business is beyond me. After everything that happened, that still feels like the biggest mystery.

I got to Sturgeon on a quiet little summer afternoon and followed the street signs to the address Cheryl had given me. The trail led me downhill, along a street that seemed to spiral inward, to the low side of town by the river, in a neighborhood with lots of broken glass lying around everywhere. Everything seemed sunken in, like the land had rotted out beneath this part of town, collapsed like a deflating basketball, yet still somehow left most of the buildings standing.

Soon as my walk leveled out, a stringy-haired, greasy guy in a tank-top and sweat pants, who must have weighed in at five hundred pounds, zipped around the corner in an electric wheelchair and almost ran my ass over. He jerked to a stop, grunted drunkenly up at me, then swerved and sped across the pocked, lumpy street without so much as a hello. He sputtered to a stop next to a ten-year-old boy who looked like an Asian version of Christopher Robin from the old Winnie the Pooh cartoons. I glanced at them talking to each other while I walked on. Before I got far, Christopher

Robin ran to catch up with me and asked if I had any change. I gave him a buck. He ran back across the street and handed it to Roller Blob. I walked to the end of the block. On the next one over was a fenced-in basketball court. I looked again at the street sign, looked at the building numbers, and checked the slip of paper with the address on it in my pocket. I looked around again and grimaced in discouragement.

This was more of a residential area – and a sad, sick one, literally sinking, probably into some abyss or other – than someplace where you went looking for a lively bar like the place Cheryl had described.

That's 'cause she was fucking with you, dumbass, my brain tried to tell me again. *Oh, baby, I've missed you so much,* I thought of her lilting voice trilling ethereally in my ear, *I love you, I love you, I love you, never run away again, it'll be different this time, baby!*

Right. Different. This time, all she'd done was keep me around long enough to scratch the ol' itch for her, right before she sent me off on a snipe-hunt into this shit, something to distract me while she ditched our motel room for points unknown and left me holding the bill. Sure, she'd known how to talk it up so it sounded legit. At least she really remembered that much from the old days.

No, that's not how she is. She was crazy and cruel back then, but look what you first found her in the middle of. She'll still be there when you get back.

Problem was, whenever I started to rethink my situation rationally, I felt that lingering soreness in my pelvis from the last time she rode me like a mad bull as if she had to fight to stay on. I saw those oily golden curls bobbing around those otherworldly green eyes, felt and smelled and tasted the milky, preternatural fragrance of those limbs, that neck, those breasts...everything I saw while I stared up into her eyes while I strained not to come too fast, every strange thing she whispered to me while we lay together afterwards. From there, all the crazy things she told me seemed easier to believe.

Don't think about her right now. Keep your brain serious. For your own sake and hers.

Still, after half another sweaty, smelly block, sweltering in that heat, I was closer to accepting my black suspicions as fact and calling it a loss to cut. Then I glanced to my left and spotted the porch of a peeling blue-gray tenement building, with neon signs for Rolling Rock and Pabst in the dim, curtained front windows. Enough paint hadn't chipped off the sign so that you could still read *The River* there, if you already knew that's what it was supposed to say. The place did have a river behind it, after all. I hoped that wasn't what they pumped the tap water out of, though after seeing the rest of the street, I wondered.

I climbed the porch and glanced back at the street in case anyone was watching. All I saw were some greasy kids on their way into the basketball court. The big ugly one covered in boiling pimples I could see from here – every pack of dirt-water small-town slum-kid punks has one – might have been giving me the mutually paranoid stink-eye. Or maybe he was glaring at Roller Blob, who buzzed on by. Asian Christopher Robin skipped along behind him, never far away apparently. I guess those two were friends, of what sort not my problem. I shrugged and went into the bar.

The place didn't take cards, but there was a sign saying there was an ATM at the convenience store around the corner. That was nice of them, but I had cash in my pocket, and couldn't let myself get drunk enough to blow it all anyway. There was a pool table and a jukebox, the old-fashioned kind that also didn't take cards and had booklets of albums under glass that flipped with the press of a button. I got a PBR from the lobster-red old guy behind the counter. He wore a checkered shirt, green suspenders, and a Korean War Vet Navy cap. When he gave me my change, I left him a dollar, went to the jukebox, and put on lots of Willie, Waylon and Coe, then returned to my seat.

"It gotten any cooler out there yet?" said the old guy.

When he said more than three words at a time, he actually sounded friendly. He had a way of going about his business with his mouth open but tightly scrunched, with crooked, sharp-looking front teeth and beady eyes, so he always looked angry from stress.

I wiped sweat from my forehead. "If it did before I got here, I don't wanna know what you were out there in earlier."

"You really don't," he said. "You just step outside to come here?"

"Just got into town. Say, how's Ethel been these days?"

He peered at me. "I seen you in here before?"

"Yeah," I lied, "a while back. We're old buddies, Ethel and me."

"Huh." He looked me over and nodded slowly. "Yeah, she should be here in a couple hours or so. Don't know if you have anywhere to be..."

"Not a damn place but here," I sighed heavily, like I'd just gotten to the end of a long day at work, as opposed to just starting one.

"Huh. Well, let me know if you need anything."

I spotted a small kitchen menu on the wall behind him and realized I was hungry. I ordered a BLT because it was the cheapest sandwich. Turned out, it wasn't bad. A few more people drifted in. I found some guys to shoot pool with, and I drank a few more beers. No less than three drunk assholes tried to start fights with me. *Offered to fight* is probably a better way to put it. Every time, I let them know I was up for it, and they all backed right off. Other than that, I was just one more days-unshaved guy in a cheap suit, hiding from the afternoon in a dark hole in the wall, with cheap beer and a jukebox with a good classic country music selection. I kept an eye on the clock. The further it got past that first hour, the closer I hung to the bar.

Eventually a tall, leathery, impossibly thin woman came in, with the longest, silkiest, whitest hair I've ever seen. She went behind the bar and started yelling at the bartender. She kept calling him Pete. Her beady eyes were identical to his. Between that, the other, smaller features they shared, and the way they bickered, I pegged them for brother and sister.

When they finished bickering, I went up and said, "Hey, Ethel!" She turned and looked at me. Before she could ask who I was or if she knew me, I said, "Wow, how long's it been since this place was called *Dave's Place*?" That's what Cheryl told me to say.

Right on cue, Ethel's hatchet face split into a grin and those dark, beady eyes turned into little upside-down rainbows of joy. "Well hello there, sweetie! Didn't recognize you at first in this bad light, and my eyes are shot to shit right now from that glaring sun out there." She came around the bar and gave me a big hug. "How's Cheryl? She around here anywhere with you?"

"Nah, she couldn't get out on the road with me this time. Her own work, you know."

"Aw, yeah, sure."

Ethel went back behind the bar, got a drink for herself, and insisted on giving me my next one on the house. We sat there for a good ten or fifteen minutes pretending we knew each other, telling each other old stories about Cheryl. I found out some interesting stories about my gal there, let me tell you. I sure looked forward to talking to her all about them.

Ethel finally said, "Listen, sweetie, I'd love to sit and keep chattin', but there's a big ol' order out there that I gotta haul in here."

"Oh, no problem. Want a hand with that?"

"Aw, sweetie, you're too much." She slapped me on the shoulder. "That'd be just wonderful."

We went out to her car, which was parked around the corner next to the convenience store with the ATM. I spent the next few minutes helping her haul in the place's latest restock of booze. Pete didn't help because the place was filling up by now, and he couldn't get away from the bar. Once we had the shipment in, Ethel grabbed one of the sixers of Ice House. She said we should go upstairs, chat, and hang out a while, "catch up on old times."

I followed her behind a curtain that led into a narrow hallway with warped boards and crooked corners. It smelled of lime and piss. We took an even sketchier flight of stairs up to a square, sparsely furnished room. Two windows faced the street, blazing in like twin rectangular magnesium flares, like a nuclear bomb had just gone off outside. That was the only light source, and it mostly just made everything in here look dimmer. It was about as hot in here as it was out there, and muggier, so all the sinister rotting smells came out to play from between the cracks in the plaster and floorboards. There was a couch in one corner with a little stand passing for a coffee table in front of it, an icebox in another, and a dresser between those magnesium-flare windows, lined on top in framed photographs of people who were probably all long dead by now. On the far right wall stood a lonely door that might be a broom or coat closet, except it was held shut with a padlock.

Ethel closed the front door. When I turned back, her whole manner had changed. Her shoulders had straightened out so she looked even taller, and her face was all stern, weary business. She set down the sixer of Ice House, without either opening one for herself or offering me one. "Well, I'll tell you this much," she said, "you're a step up from what she usually sends."

"Ma'am?"

"Don't call me *ma'am*. Oh sure, I might be old enough to hear it, but you're sure as shit too young to be sayin' it."

"I'm older than I look."

"Oh, don't give me that shit. Who the hell says *ma'am* anymore, anyway? It's like an outhouse in an elevator. It don't belong. Anyhow, maybe the same goes for you. You really seem like a nice young fella. That's too bad, but that's her business. I guess she told you how this goes from here?"

"She did." I stopped myself from saying *ma'am* again.

"So wanna get on with reporting what she has to report from out there, so I can send you back with whatever she needs to know for the next couple months?"

"First I'd like to make sure I'm talking to the right person."

"Excuse me?" She looked at me like I'd told a dirty joke that was over the line.

"I wanna see the room before I tell you anything."

"You got some sass, don't you?"

"Hey, you know how it is. I was sent to see between Cheryl and Ethel's business like a professional. Professionals pay attention to details."

She looked me over and sighed. "Yeah, sure. Sure, why not." She smirked ironically. "I don't see the harm."

She dug through her pants pocket on her way to the locked closet door. Doing both at once made her shoulder and hip tighten. She looked like she was still in pain when she bent to fiddle with the padlock, like an old giant who'd grown bent and broken from a life spent trapped in a world full of things built too small for them.

When I followed her over, she splayed her free palm my way and went, "Hey! Just hold your horses a second." The padlock fell away, into her other palm. The door swung open. At first, from where I stood, it was dark as a broom closet, bigger, but otherwise unremarkable. "Well, come on now," she said with a beckoning wave, like calling a dog.

I went and looked, over her shoulder at first. She eased to the side, as though giving me permission to step past her for a better look. I did. It took even longer for my eyes to adjust this time. The only light still came from the windows behind us, or so it seemed at first. It was a little bare, rectangular room, with no light fixtures, just a giant starfish of out-of-control black mold that bloomed from the center of the floor, with blotchy arms spreading out, climbing the walls and speckling out across the ceiling. My nose stung like someone had punched me in it. Little multi-hued gleaming spots speckled the mold all over, like thousands of precious gems and stones stuck in it. My eyes widened as they adjusted. Those speckles gave off more than enough of their own light, because they weren't stones.

The black, inky spread pulsed and roiled from deep within, like a three-dimensional painting. I stared at the center of the black growth, which wasn't any kind of growth at all, more like an interdimensional rip in the fabric of reality of the walls and floorboards, showing some churning, alien nebula. Deep down, down, down in that place, something stirred, uncoiled, and slithered up through the extraterrestrial sea, towards us...towards me. It seemed made of the blackness of the nebula, a purer concentration of it, yet I could already make out some of the speckled patterns on its massive form, like I'd been able to see the boiling pimples on the big ugly punk kid outside from a distance. This being was a lot farther away than that guy had been. As it drew nearer, its eyes opened and looked into mine.

"So you satisfied with what you see?" Ethel said behind me.

"Oh yes, ma'am. I sure am."

"Good." She didn't even object this time when I called her ma'am, I noticed. She just stepped back quickly through the doorway and tried to slam it shut on me.

She didn't expect me to be ready for that, certainly not for me grab her by one of those long arms and yank so she stumbled forward into the closet. I don't think she ever noticed the box-cutter in my hand, either. I made sure she'd careened well past me before I cut her throat, so most of the spray missed me. It gushed out like floodwater from a storm drain, into the nebulous rift...not splattering *on it*, pouring *into it*. All the stars and galaxies in there flared to life, so bright that I saw their rising, uncoiling king's jaws open to catch the hot spill. He, or she, or it rose faster, more eagerly.

Ethel landed with her back half on the bare boards, her front half dangling into the abyss. The big thing rose faster, hungrier, towards her. So did a lot of smaller things I couldn't make out so well, like a school of hungry little fish, swarming around the big fish and following it to dinner. I fished the Zippo from my pocket, flicked it open, sparked the flame to life, and tossed it into the center of the inky, alien spread. It turned to a fiery gust like their whole universe in there was made of some combustible gas. The flames roared up at me. The heat wave hit me in the face. I jumped back through the door and slammed it shut before the flames themselves could roar out into the room and get me.

I didn't know if that other place would eat all the flames that cauterized the rift shut, or if this world would have to deal with them on this side, too. I'd just done what Cheryl had pleaded for me to come here and do. The door shook from the other side as I pressed my shoulder to it and got the padlock back on it. Greenish smoke flooded from beneath the door around my feet. By the time I snapped the padlock into place properly, the metal was already almost too hot to handle. By the time I made it back to the hallway, the green smoke had filled up the room.

I reached the staircase and started down. Pete, the bartender, Ethel's brother, was on his way up. Those beady eyes of his were already wide with comprehending fury. Right as I was thinking he looked decrepit enough that he shouldn't be hard to get through, he reached behind him and pulled a gun from the waistband of his jeans. I dove beneath the gun as he aimed.

I don't know if the shot went off before or after I caught him around the ankles. All I know is, my ears didn't stop ringing for a few hours afterwards. My hands, once they were free, kept patting at my torso, expecting to feel my shirt wet with blood, over a fresh gunshot wound that hadn't yet doubled me up in agony because of the adrenaline. I kept catching myself doing that for weeks afterwards, whenever I heard something that sounded like a gunshot or I saw someone get shot on TV.

By the time I rose up over Pete, I still didn't know for sure whether or not I'd been shot, just that I could still stand and he couldn't. The gun was still in his hand. He groaned and tried to lift it, so I stomped on his wrist. He groaned again, louder, and looked up at me hatefully like he might shout loud enough to bring other troublemakers. I stomped a few more times, this time on his face, frantically, like on a poisonous bug that just wouldn't go *squish*. His skull didn't exactly go squish, more collapsed and sagged into a slightly different shape, like a melon breaking inside a tight sack. Pink and gray and purple fluid squirted out of his ears. For a second, my chest thundered so hard that I couldn't move, while my skull felt like it was on a rollercoaster. Not being able to move is bad, when there are smoke and flames at your back, and you don't know who's gonna come in from what other direction at any second, and there's an old man at your feet who you just turned into a corpse, and not in a nice way.

No one came into the little hallway after Pete, and I managed to pull myself together. I almost went back the way I'd come in, but had sense left to know it wouldn't be good to leave through the bar. I ran down another, shorter hallway, and found another exit, through the side.

By the time I found my way back out onto the street, the five-hundred pound man in the electric wheelchair was zipping up and down the other side of the street, shouting hysterically for someone named Gustav. He spotted me walking fast and buzzed across the street to me. He asked me frantically if I'd seen his nephew. I guess he meant Asian Christopher Robin, so I said no and walked on. He buzzed after me, caught up with me, and asked me a few more times if I'd seen Gustav.

Finally I shouted, "No, I haven't seen Christopher Robin! Now fuck off." After that, either he got the message, or I walked fast enough to get the hell away from him.

It was later, so it was cooler out. Black smoke and red and yellow flame spilled from the upper windows, along the whole block by now. I recognized some folks pouring out of the bar downstairs into the cracked winding street. I'd shot pool with a few of them in there earlier. I hadn't told anyone my real name. Sure, they saw me talking to Ethel, and she introduced me to a couple of them as an old friend. Ethel talked to a lot of people in that place, and she had a lot of old friends. The punk kids I'd seen earlier now stood together gawking from the edge of the basketball court. No one looked at me. Any forensic evidence linking me to the place went up in flames, I kept telling myself. The terrible scene dropped away in the distance as I hoofed it uphill. Everything else was weirdly quiet.

I said before how that scuzzy part of town seemed sunken in, right, like the ground was slowly rotting out beneath it? Well, as I walked uphill out of it, it seemed more and more like I could *feel* it sinking, faster and faster. At the time, I told myself it was my worked-up nerves. I crossed the tracks into the part of town that was alive and bright with normal summer small-town night life. No one was going crazy up here, so I guess word hadn't spread that half a block had caught fire on the other side of town.

As I walked back to my car, some fresh pep filled my step, thinking about Cheryl. She'd been right, my beautiful Cheryl. Everything she'd told me would happen had happened, and then some. Now we were free.

I got back to where I'd parked, out of sight in a small lot behind an alleyway. I sat in the driver's seat sobering up a little before I pulled out, got back on the interstate, and went back to the motel an hour away, where she said she'd wait for me.

When I got there, I found a note on the bed, next to a stack of money.

Sean,

Thank you so much, more than you could ever know. Also believe me when I say I didn't lie when I said I love you, even though you'll probably hate me after this, at least for a long time. I hope you live long enough to at least get some perspective on things. If you never get the happy memories back – I hope you do – I hope you at least come to understand enough to forgive me a little. When I said I wanted to go home, I meant it. There's a reason I never actually told you where home was exactly. When I said I needed you to go do what you did before I could, that part was true. If you're reading this, you've seen what I mean. I also meant it when I said I wanted you to come with me. I just never said I could take you with me. I'm sorry I had to mislead you, but like you said yourself, I knew you were someone who could do the job. That room was the seal that Ethel as she called herself was guarding, and I couldn't go home until it burned. What you saw in that room, that wasn't home, in case that's what you're thinking. That was the home of my family's enemies. I'm on my way home now, and I'll never forget you.

Love always, through worlds and ages,
Cheryl

My lovely Cheryl...Yeah, now everything about you makes a little more sense, from your strange fragrance to the stranger things you used to whisper in bed. I love you too. Now you're on your way, and so am I. Sure, yeah, thanks for everything.

I counted the money she left. The next day, in another motel in another state, I read in the news how a whole low-side section of a little Vermont town had collapsed and sunken into a marshland so the dirty nearby river had flowed in and claimed it. The article mentioned a big tenement fire that had broken out shortly before the occurrence, but that was mostly a footnote, in light of the larger freak of nature. The article said the ground in that area had been slowly sinking for years, so it had always been a matter of time, but no one had figured out why it had all happened so suddenly, all at once. One scientist mentioned something about some weird kind of unidentified black mold that lived everywhere in the new swampland.

Well, I couldn't say Cheryl had been up front with me about everything, but at least she hadn't shorted me on the bill for the motel.

Kids Say The Weirdest Things

Our neighbors are nice, but a little weird. That's okay. So are we. A few months ago, my husband and I moved into the middle of a three-unit townhouse in a little country village. Spring turned into summer fast, and I'm getting back into shape turning part of the back yard into a little vegetable garden.

The neighbors to our left are quiet and mostly keep to themselves. It's the ones to the right that I wonder about. There's a single mom with a teenage daughter and a cute little boy who's maybe six or seven. The boy has a friend who often comes over and plays, a bouncy little girl his age from down the road. Some nights the lady has some friends over. They play strange music. I've only seen her friends a couple times, showing up and leaving while I'm out on the back porch with insomnia and a cigarette. The lady and her kids don't look or act wealthy, but their friends must be, judging by those fine tailored black suits they always wear. Sometimes they sing along to the music. It's muffled through the walls, not too bothersome, but I do notice. It sounds like some foreign language I can't place. So it's funny that they occasionally complain about the noise my husband makes when he's up late drinking and writing.

STORY TIME WITH CRAZY UNCLE MATT

The other day, I was out in the garden. It had been a dry couple of weeks, and I sighed in irritation at the wilting edges of the kale and squash I was trying to grow. I thought about using the hose, even though the lady next door would complain about how that drains the well. An SUV pulled into the driveway. I looked up and saw our neighbor get out. She crossed the back yard, to her back porch. Her little boy followed. I remembered them leaving earlier. They'd both been dressed up nice when they left, like they were going to some fancy occasion. I'm pretty sure the boy's little friend from down the road was with them when they left. She wasn't with them now. The mom was still dressed up fancy, but her son now wore plain shorts and a sports T-shirt. He ambled sullenly behind her, like he'd been bad and gotten scolded or spanked. They climbed the steps and went inside. A few minutes later, the mom came back out. She'd changed into shorts, flip-flops, and a tank-top. She started seeing to her flower boxes on her back porch. Before long, the little boy came out and joined her. He looked happier now, scampering and hopping and laughing around, enjoying life like little kids ought to in the summer out in the country, on a day like today. I glanced up with bored interest semi-regularly, from beneath the shadow of my floppy straw sunhat.

Up on the porch, the boy squealed at his mom, "Can I go out and see her?"

I glanced at my struggling crop. The leaves didn't look half so wilted as they had earlier. Maybe it was the light, but they looked like they'd gone a few shades darker green.

I didn't realize the kid was talking about me 'til I heard his Mom say, "No, no, she's busy."

"Please? I wanna go see her! I *like* her!"

My husband was at work, I'd been at my gardening for a while, and I thought overhearing that was so adorable, so I went *What the hell?* "It's okay," I called out, tilting my chin up and putting on my best smile. "He can come say hi!"

His mom said something like, "Okay, you can go say hi, but don't bother her too much."

With a big grin on his face, he bounded down and raced out across the back yard towards me. I kept seeing to my gardening. He trotted to a halt and stood there watching me, like I was the most fascinating thing in the world.

"Hi, how you doing?" I said.

"I'm okay," he said. "I like you."

"I like you too," I said with a giggle.

"Guess what! We went to church today!"

"Is that right?" Oh, yeah, today was Sunday. I hadn't figured them for the church-going sort of family – whatever that is anymore since I was a kid – but okay.

"Yeah. Me, my mom, and Susie."

"Is Susie your little friend I always see you with?" His teenage sister was named Kelly or something. She was out of town this week with some friends, I think I remember hearing. Spring break, or something.

"Yeah," he said.

"What church you guys go to?"

"The one up the dirt road over there." He pointed off to the road that ran down to the left of the house, past a few barns and houses.

"Oh, you mean the one back that way, through the woods?"

"Uh-huh."

"Oh, neat! I've seen that place when I've been out on

bike rides. That's a pretty church." It really is a lovely building, the one we were talking about, the old arching colonial sort of structure. "I didn't know we knew anyone who goes there."

"Uh-huh, and today the Priest had me and Susie help him with the ceremony."

Priest? Ceremony? That was a little surprising. I guess I'd just assumed in the back of my mind that the place was something Protestant, so they'd have a pastor or preacher or reverend or whatever. I hadn't seen any Catholic churches around here. Episcopalian, maybe?

I just said, "Wow, cool."

"Yeah. It was a special ceremony, because it's a special day, and the priest said we're special. He put the high scepters at the end of big, long poles, and had us hold them, one of us on each side of him."

"Wow, that's really great! You must be really, really proud and excited."

"Yeah! And you know what else? The priest asked me and Susie which of us wanted to walk in front of him and which one wanted to walk behind him. I wanted to go first, but Susie said she wanted to go first too. So I, I, I let Susie go first. Mom tells me I'm a gentleman. The Priest called me a little gentleman too, so I...I...I wanted to be a gentleman to Susie."

"Well, it sounds like you are, and that's good," I said. "You should keep being a gentleman. Not enough men are."

"Yeah. Do you want to hear about what we did at church?"

I really didn't, but I still said, "Yeah, keep telling me!"

"The Priest, he...he...Once we walked up to the altar,

the Priest had me and Susie stand...one on each side of him...up at the...the altar. The Priest read words from the Great Old Book."

"Oh, you mean the Bible?"

"No. The Great Old Book. Anyway, the Priest had me and Susie stand on each side of him while he read the words in the Great Old Book. We were both holding the high scepters up, so the tops of them were above his head while he read. That's a real special thing. Then because Susie walked in front up to the altar, the Priest picked her up and he put her on the altar. The Priest had me help him open Susie up and take things out of her. It was...was...It was really scary when Susie screamed. But then she went to sleep, and it wasn't scary anymore. It started smelling bad after she stopped screaming. The...the Priest said she was asleep. I was glad she got to sleep. Oh, oh, and then me and the Priest took things out of Susie and put them all around the altar, like the Great Old Book told the Priest how to do. The Priest kept saying words from the Great Old Book while we took stuff out of Susie and we...we...spread her around.

"Then all the lights in the church went kinda dark. So did the lights in the window. The rest of the people out in the benches were saying stuff with us. There were things outside the windows. The things had wings like birds, except they weren't birds, and they had wings like flying dinosaurs have, but they weren't dinosaurs either. They had big wings, and...and...the big things kept flapping their wings on the windows outside. You know what else? It was really messy when we arranged Susie's insides around. Big millipedes came out of the red mess that came out of Susie. The big millipedes took the rest of Susie away. They also took some of the people out in the benches away. The Priest said it was because their faith was weak, but that's good the millipedes took them away too, because now the land of this town is cleaned up of them, and now the town can live on out here for another year.

"You're gonna grow lots of good stuff in your garden now. The dirt's gonna be really, really good all summer, because of what me and Susie and the Priest did when we stood at the altar, and the Priest said the words so the Ones Who Rule The Woods won't be mad at us now for another summer. I'm sad because I won't get to play with Susie for a while anymore."

I didn't know what to say to all that. I guess I just stared at him.

He saw me frowning, and he put his hands in his pockets, and shuffled around like he felt guilty, like it dawned on him that he shouldn't have told me about all that. He met my eyes again, pouted for a second, then turned and ran back across the yard, up his porch, and into the house.

Not knowing what to make of all that, I took another look at my garden's yieldings. Now that the little guy mentioned it, the kale looked twice as full as before, and my squashes had swelled and ripened already.

No One Rides For Free

Everett Kale looked up and down the lonely highway, along both strips of the lonely crossroads, between the tall pines beneath the deepening sky. Jimmy kept glancing back, spooked by every little night-noise as the trees behind them grew blacker with dusk.

Everett sloshed his cold coffee around in the paper to-go cup from the diner. Jimmy started yammering again. Everett told him to shut up, again. Everett was just glad he'd gotten Jimmy out of the diner when he had, before Jimmy had gotten both their asses kicked by all those good ol' boys in the place, for hitting on that teenage waitress. She'd been cute and perky, Everett had to admit. He'd ignored Jimmy's antics and tried to enjoy his biscuits and gravy, then he'd spotted some unwelcome grab-ass happening, which he wasn't okay with. This was what he got, he figured, for taking up with a sex-offender fresh out of prison as a road-dog.

At least Everett had gotten them both to the crossroads by sunset. All Jimmy wanted was to get to his sister's up north in the next few days. She'd promised to let him crash there a while, with her and the kids, he said. His sister knew all the charges were bullshit, he said.

"Yeah, sure, whatever, man," Everett answered over and over.

He went on watching the scant traffic, didn't put his thumb out for every car or truck that passed. He knew what kind to watch for...mostly old models, with a special kind of scuff built up over their frames, with young-looking silhouettes behind the wheel. Everett had someplace he needed to get to as well, by roughly this time tomorrow night. If things went liked he hoped, he'd get a nice fat wad of cash for his trouble, enough to maybe take some time off from this kind of shit. One thing at a time, though...

Everett knew this area. He knew the kinds of folks that liked to cruise along this way, past sunset...the right ones, anyhow. They'd be along sooner or later. If someone of no use to him stopped first...well, he'd figure something out.

Finally, a long, black '54 hot rod sprayed gravel as it pulled onto the shoulder next to them. Three folks sat inside, two up front, one in back.

The front passenger window rolled down. "Hey, guys," said the crisp, sweet twang. "Where you headed?"

Everett strutted forward. "Oh, northwards," he answered, before Jimmy could say anything.

"Holy shit," said the young-looking woman in the front passenger seat, "is that Everett Kale?"

"That Sturge?" Everett did his best to sound just as surprised as she did.

Theodora Sturgeon batted her dark eyelashes. "It sure is, handsome. You and your friend there just climb right on into the back."

"Hey, now hold on," said the younger-looking guy in the driver's seat, the one with the goatee and the ponytail, wearing all black leather.

"Cool it, Frank," said Sturge. "We're headed north already, right? Climb on in, boys."

Everett peered at the guy in the driver's seat. What do you know, bad ol' Franklin Fuckin' Fairfax Secorea, still fuming with all the same old hot-shit attitude. Whatever. The scrawny punk couldn't have been older than sixteen when he'd died and come back, however many centuries ago, and in Everett's estimation, that went for mentally as well as physically. After a century or two in America, only a hint of the old Irish accent lingered.

With a shrug, Everett let Jimmy climb into the back first. Jimmy shivered, hopped in, and scooted over next to a pretty, creamy-faced, heavyset woman. She had blue eyes with thick blue eyeliner, wore blue jeans and a lacy robin's-egg-blue top. Everett got in next to Jimmy, sandwiching him in, and slammed the door. The car took off down the lonely highway, through the night.

"Okay, boys," sighed Frank, his pale, spidery fingers tense on the wheel, "where you headed?"

"Perkinsville," said Everett. "I got me some business up there...I figure...oh, by around this time tomorrow night."

"Hey, wait a minute..." Jimmy started.

"Relax, buddy." Everett clapped Jimmy on the shoulder. "My old pals here, they got us covered. Didn't I tell you you'd be all set, takin' up with me on the road?"

Jimmy looked around. "Wait, wait...You...you...know these people?"

"Shit, yeah!" Everett slapped his knee. "Ain't it funny, how sometimes ol' Lady Luck decides to give you some road-head. Ain't that right, Sturge?"

Sturge looked back at Everett, lashing a wild mane of lush dark hair, flashing a voluptuous, sharp-toothed smile from a pale, heart-shaped face. "Oh, that's right, baby," she said.

Frank's hands tightened on the wheel and they sped up some. "Yeah, but you got something to pay with, right, fellas? You know the saying. *Ass, gas or grass, nobody rides for free.*"

"Oh, I've got a payment for you," said Everett. He winked at Sturge through the dashboard mirror.

Sturge caught his look, winked back, and licked her lips. She rubbed Frank's shoulder, leaned towards him, purred in his ear, "Aw, come on, honey, you know Everett, right?"

"Yeah," Frank grumbled, keeping his eyes fixed on the road. "I sure as hell do."

"Yeah," said Everett, "so you know I always make good. Relax, ol' buddy. You're still the one in the driver's seat."

"You're Goddamn right," Frank muttered.

"Baby, relax." Sturge's hand slid across Frank's chest, then drifted lower as she leaned in. "We can talk about payment when we stop to rest."

Frank pressed the gas a little harder. The yellow lines in the middle of the road sped by a little blurrier in the hot rod's headlights. "Yeah," he rasped. "Sure."

Frank's pointy fingers reached out and turned a knob, so the classic country music station on the radio blared a little louder. Everett sang along to Johnny Cash, Willie Nelson and Merle Haggard, 'til Frank growled at him to shut the fuck up, and Sturge purred at Frank to take it easy. Jimmy periodically made awkward attempts to get to know everybody, interjecting himself into various conversations. A few times he flirted halfheartedly with the blue lady next to him. She mostly ignored him.

Everett popped the plastic top off his coffee cup and gulped the last of the cold, black swill. He held up the cup. "Got anywhere you want me to toss this?"

"Man, you looked around at this mess?" said Sturge. "Just toss it on the floor somewhere."

Everett tossed the cup on the floor at his feet, along with the lid. He kept most of his real thoughts to himself. That was usually best around these kinds of folks...these kinds of *critters*, more accurately...more than one of them, anyhow. Sure, he got it. Sturge was with Frank these days, or nights, rather. What did Everett have to complain about? If him and Sturge hooked up now, after all this time, he'd look like almost as big of a pederast as Jimmy, never mind how she'd be the cougar in the mix, which come to think of it, she always had been. Maybe you could call it shallowness, passing up his chance with her when he had. Whatever. He had his own business in Perkinsville. Frank had already promised to get him there on time. Plus these folks didn't ask questions.

After a few hours and piss-stops, the first glimmer of dawn bled faintly through the sky. Frank drove next to it 'til he spotted the right kind of out-of-the-way spot and jerked the car to a halt, far from the roadside, under and behind some thick brush and low-hanging branches. He shifted into park, unbuckled his seat belt, twisted around, and peered at Everett with silver-coin catlike eyes. "Okay, man. I think it's time we talked about payment."

Everett clapped and squeezed Jimmy's shoulder. "You know damn well. I got this guy right here."

The pretty, heavy-set blue girl opened her sharp-toothed mouth and clamped her jaws shut hard on the side of Jimmy's throat. The breath went out of him before he could scream. In the murky, shrouded dawn, the welling flood around her lips looked black. Frank twisted around and crawled over the top of his seat like a cat. He caught one of Jimmy's flailing arms, pushed back the dirty sleeve, and bit down on the wrist. Sturge made it easier on herself by pulling the lever so her seat dropped backwards with a rusty whine. She slithered forward on her belly, caught one of Jimmy's kicking legs by the knee, pressed it down gently, pushed his thighs apart, then ripped at his jeans so she could get at his femoral artery. On her way there, she crawled over Everett. He couldn't resist copping a little feel, which she didn't seem to mind. In fact, she flexed herself deeper into his touch, writhed and undulated against him while she drank her fill from Jimmy's inner thigh.

For Everett, it was a bittersweet few minutes. It wasn't easy, holding still with a sudden, raging adrenaline boner. Feeling Sturge writhe against him, spotting her mouth getting more and more red-smeared, he almost wished he was Jimmy. Then he noticed what the other two were doing to the poor bastard, so he thought better of it. He also reminded himself that if he did anything to piss these folks off right now, he'd be next, deal or no. That didn't do a thing to ease his adrenaline boner.

The whole time, there were all the old mixed feelings, about decisions it was too late to take back. Making the long haul with Sturge would have meant letting her turn him into her kind of critter. He'd tried the whole blood-drinking thing once, before he even knew for sure that critters like Sturge existed for real. It just wasn't for him. Blood tasted nasty, so he couldn't get into the idea of spending eternity with the stuff as a primary dietary necessity. Plus, sucking down that much spurting blood from an open main-vein without it going all over the place? It was worse than a damn keg-stand! How did Sturge and the others put up with it, all the time, night after night, decade after decade, century after century?

Jimmy stopped twitching. Sturge and the others slid free of him like glutted, bloated leeches. Frank and the blue girl slumped in a pile together on the floor of the back seat. Sturge tried to sit up, then fell sideways against Everett. She moaned, grumbled, snaked an arm across his chest, and flopped her head on his shoulder. He was glad her lips didn't fall too close to his neck. That didn't change how nice she felt right now. He let one arm drape around her, caressed her shoulder, and otherwise kept his hands to himself, like a gentleman. Mostly. As the sun rose, he cradled her and, for a while, imagined himself in one perfect, serene moment of an alternate lifetime, where everything had turned out differently.

After a while, Everett opened his door and eased out from under Sturge. He got out, stretched, leaned in and gave her a little kiss on the cheek, then went around to the other side of the car. Before he opened the door, he noticed Frank and the blue girl slumped against it from the inside. He lifted the lever slowly, tried to reach in quickly enough so they didn't fall out, but they still did. He winced, half expecting them to wake up and get pissed. No, they just hung there, only partly fallen out, their hair smearing the dirt, like two rag dolls that snored. At least that made it easier to haul out what was left of Jimmy.

Jesus H Fuck, these bastards had really sucked Jimmy's ass dry, to where his stinky clothes hung an extra size too large over his shriveled frame. Everett dragged the bone-dry husk out of the car and into the leaves. He hauled it up over his shoulder and carried it off deep into the woods. Before leaving it in a gulch for the birds and bugs, he checked all the pockets for spare cash. Just his luck, all the bastard had was a couple bucks and some change.

Everett got back to the car, lifted Frank and the blue girl back inside, and leaned them against each other. He climbed into the front passenger seat that Sturge had already leaned back. He didn't wake 'til the sun was setting. By then, the others were already up.

Sturge was shaking him. "Hey, buddy. My seat. Only I ride shotgun around here."

"Where's dipshit?" said the blue girl. Everett still hadn't caught her name.

"Hey, man, thanks for getting rid of the leftovers," said Frank as they got back on the road.

"No problem, man," said Everett. "Guess y'all didn't mind the fare I paid?"

"Yeah, sure, it'll do, for now," said Frank. "Where'd you say you needed to go?"

"Perkinsville," said Everett as he buckled his seat belt. "Little place, right on the edge of town as you pass through. You can't miss it. I'll let you know where to stop."

Frank gunned it and they sped off through the fresh, young night. This time when Everett sang along with the radio, Sturge sang along with him, to Tom Waits' *Ol' 55*. When Frank told them to shut the fuck up, Sturge stuck her tongue out at him and they went on crooning along together with Hank Williams.

They dropped Everett off outside a little farmhouse with a tailgate party raging outside. He said goodbye to everyone and walked downhill towards it. The black hot rod full of blood-sucking fiends sped off down the road, into the night. Everett hadn't asked about their business elsewhere, because he honestly didn't care. If anything interesting happened, Sturge would tell him all about it, next time they had a chance to catch up.

The blood-sucking fiends had never asked Everett Kale about his business, because they just plain didn't want to know. It was better that way, for everyone.

Have Some Dragon's Blood

Nick just had to check the shop out. The name alone required a look. Above tapestries of black, purple and gold, there ran the banner of black Gothic letters spelling *The Old French Bastard*. Tribal sculptures sat behind the glass, on a bed of polished pebbles. When he went in, the place was so dark and still that he wondered if the owner had forgotten to turn the sign around or lock up. Incense he didn't recognize filled the air, heady and...not musky, more like hot perfumed flesh in a foreign whorehouse. For some reason, it also reminded him of things he didn't like remembering.

The harsh hanging lamp above the counter didn't cast enough light, but Nick had great night vision. Archaic weapons covered the right wall, from medieval swords to Wild West six-shooters. Next to it were a few used clothes racks. Otherwise, it was mostly conventional antiques like furniture, oil paintings and jewelry. Under glass beneath the register were fancy cigarette cases, whiskey flasks, glass and ceramic pipes.

Nick peered over the counter, through a curtain into a back room, but he still couldn't see or hear anyone. Three incense sticks bristled from a long brass burner on the counter like porcupine quills with glowing tips. They were blood red, and yes, blood was what the smell reminded him of...blood laced with spices from weirder, further ports than any he'd seen or heard of.

As he eyed an old kukri knife that looked ancient enough to have killed men in battle, movement sounded behind him.

"My apologies, young sir." A small hunched old man now stood behind the counter, with gleaming white hair, thick arching brows and pale beady eyes above a sly smile. The accent told Nick where the store's name came from. "Did you need assistance?"

"No. I wondered if anyone was here, though."

"No, my business has not yet been *unmanned by the raptures.*" The old guy's smile stretched up to one side like he was getting away with something.

Nick nodded. "Guess they keep the Bible belt strapped tight around here. How's a place like this go over?"

"Well enough to keep the lights on." The old man smiled wider, so his crooked, sharp-looking teeth gleamed pearly white in the dimness. "How does my shop *go over* for you, young friend?"

"I like it fine," said Nick. "What do you call that incense?"

"Ah, the Dragon's Blood, the finest you will find."

"Dragon's Blood, huh." Nick checked out the tubular black-painted cubicles holding the large incense selection. "Doesn't smell like any blend of Dragon's Blood incense I ever smelled."

"Ah! And did you gain an appreciation for incense overseas?"

"Huh? Oh, no, my ex fiancee burned the stuff all the time. It drove me nuts after a while, actually. I swear, she used to burn it like a chain-smoker. To be honest, I couldn't stand it then, but I like it now. It helps me relax, long as someone's not overdoing it."

"You are a man who has difficulty relaxing." There was that damn smile-stretch again. "A result of...the wartime?"

Nick's brows furrowed. It was weird to still be recognized as a soldier, more so out of nowhere by this weird little old guy. "Heh. No, but that didn't exactly help."

"You are now...on leave from our time of war?"

"No. I haven't been in the Marines since Iraq."

"Then you were...wounded in battle."

"Yeah."

"Badly?"

"Bad enough to get an honorable discharge." Nick avoided the old guy's eyes. "Look, tell me more about this fancy Dragon's Blood you got here."

"You have more than a passing interest in the nature and art of incense."

"The name makes me curious."

"Indeed. Have you seen the oil paintings I carry of dragons?"

"Yeah, those are cool. But how 'bout this you're burning?"

"Ah, yes, its history runs deep, my Dragon's Blood, through both the Oriental and the European, and beyond. You could trace it back as far as ancient Greece. Most of what you will find today – what has been the standard recipe since at least the fifteenth century – is derived from the dried red drops of the Dracaena tree of the Canary Islands and Morocco, traded into ancient Europe by the Incense Road."

"Most of?"

"Or similar, less extravagant approximations. As Unicorns are the wistful dreams of young girls, are you a boy who's not grown up, so that you continue chasing your dragons?"

"Heh. I...guess?"

"Bear in mind, young man. Those who used the incense in medieval ritual and alchemy did so believing that they burned, quite literally, *the dried blood of true dragons.* There are accounts, you know, in ancient writings known to few who live, of dragons who came forth from a dark land not of this physical realm. When the sun falls, if you know where to look, you can see the forests of that dark land spread before you. At the bidding of their flame-crowned king, dragons with scales of obsidian flew from their realm to wreak havoc in ours. A chosen few knights, versed in both the sword and...other arts...were sent forth to where the barrier lay thinnest. There a messenger from the dragon realm laid out half a circle of stones around a petrified stump, leaving the middle of the configuration open. He bid the knights walk through the opening and wait.

"As the sun set, the forest of the dark realms materialized before them. In its shadows, they searched for the weapons needed to slay the great demonic beasts. There they met with older, wiser, just dragons, from whom the obsidian beasts had hailed before they were scorched and warped by the blazing king's flame. The old wise Dragon King gave to the knights new weapons, forged, it is said, from his own scales. Once they returned home – to a world that would one day die and be reborn as our own – they slew the renegade beasts to the last. The blood of the beasts flowed across the land, soaking deep into the soil. Strange new plant life grew from it, plants that most of the people did not recognize. To those few knights who'd survived the quest and the battles that followed, however, the new growth was all too familiar."

"Huh. Making the question," Nick said, more to himself than the shopkeeper, "what part of the dragon spirit lived on in the new life that grew?"

"You mean, was it the ancient strength and wisdom of the great beasts from the further realms, or the madness and destruction that had infected the marauders?"

The obvious answer wasn't pretty. Too bad Nick couldn't blame what he'd seen of regular ol' humans, from whatever race or nation or creed, on a bunch of old dead dragons. "Yeah, and which part did all those ancient clerics and alchemists invoke?"

"Perhaps it depended entirely upon the user."

"So your Dragon's Blood incense comes from a different source than what you'll find in the average New Age shop, huh?" Nick kept his tone dry, but the alien scent already swirled through his mind, so the images of the old man's tales seemed to swirl and waft through the smoke in the strange, dim light.

In answer, the old man gave his widest, toothiest smile yet. Nick shrugged, nodded and looked around a little longer. Finally he put two dozen sticks in a long plastic baggie and laid it on the counter.

An old Miles Davis CD spun on continuous play. Nick burned incense 'til his apartment was almost as aromatic as Gloria's old place. Except Gloria had never burned anything like this. After getting knocked on his ass by some weed he'd scored off a neighbor downstairs, he checked his e-mail while his high mellowed. Ralph had sent him more pages of script for the comic they were collaborating on, on and off, Ralph writing, Nick drawing. The project was Ralph's baby, really, and he was paying Nick for the art in installments. The collaboration hadn't been as steady since Nick had moved, but it meagerly supplemented his shitty monthly disability checks and helped him keep his drawing hand sharp. He gave the script the dry cold eye he'd give a dossier. He'd find his emotional way to the setting, story, and characters once he started drawing.

Nick lit a fresh incense stick and waved it under his nose, inhaling deeply. The fumes burned, cleared his sinuses and lit up something in his brain like no drug could. Then he slid the stick into place on the burner next to his pad, a single silky gray tendril rippling up from the glowing tip.

It had taken a long time to rehabilitate himself so he could move around without looking like a stroke victim. By now he was pretty sure most folks didn't notice, except on days when the pain got really bad. He'd felt well enough when he'd gone into the shop, but the owner had still spotted it. Now that he was stoned, it mattered less. The weed, like incense, was part of his light aroma-therapeutic diet. Except tonight it wasn't relaxing...more like a new kind of restlessness, more enthusiastic, so he chased unexplored avenues of his secret inner life.

Ralph's story was about a futuristic cyberpunk Kansas City with vampires and demons running around. Tonight Nick found himself wishing there were dragons in it for him to draw. He got a full two and a half pages sketched before he couldn't concentrate and the walls blurred. When his eyes closed, he found a new, more colorful blur behind them. Miles Davis mingled with gibbering, alien nighttime wilderness sounds. The clearer the sounds grew, the more familiar they felt, like the fading music Nick knew by heart.

Within this swirl, his clothes were of leather and some unfamiliar cloth, thinner than the jeans he'd worn back in his apartment. The britches were cinched tight with twine at his waist, and a thick leather belt was slung over his shoulder, crossing his chest, sagging on his hip from a wide-bladed, long-handled sword. Beneath the clothes, his skin was slick with lumpy muck. Behind him, clanking armor drowned out the music.

When one of his comrades said something, he looked around. Through the winding maze of pulpy overhead branches, the moon was a little over half full. In a sunless land, a green, blood-veined moon was the only measure of time. Its cycle took as many hours as passed in a day in the land the knights had known, or so he'd reckoned. How many cycles had come and gone since the original seven had passed into this sweltering, growth-choked world ruled by demons?

By now, three knights remained, including himself. The party was midway up the slick slope. Light shimmered over the hilltop, from a source that must be bright as the sun they'd left behind. Many yards to the right through the trees, the hill split. Through it ran the trail they weren't supposed to have strayed from. The captain had led them off in search of food, and had quickly become food himself, to one of the hulking, gnarled beasts that ruled this jungle, the ones shaped like apes with slick warty hides like frogs, except that their skin shimmered iridescent blue. The remaining knights slew two of the beasts before the rest retreated through the trees. Desperate with hunger, the party had cut and cooked meat from the carcasses. Most of them ate reluctantly, fearing the devils' flesh may be poisonous, but not the man now in the lead, scouting with his ears. Rather, he'd gobbled ravenously, cutting off slices he ate dripping raw. Since eating of the creatures, his senses and wits felt uncannily at home here, somehow one with his settings, which made survival more likely. His devoured captain would have mingled with the meat, he noted. When he shat it out, he praised the gods – both of this land and his own – to finally be rid of the fool.

They'd not rediscovered the trail since, and the jungle had claimed three more of them. Wiping sweat from his eyes, he glanced to where the hill split. The earth leading to the crevice was smooth.

"There's the damn path finally," he muttered. Oh well, little good it did now. Their goal, by his reckoning, lay just over the hill, less trouble to simply finish the climb.

One of his companions called to him again.

"What's that?"

"I asked what you'd heard, Yeorg. And slow down."

He'd left behind the last of his armor days ago, preferring free, stealthy movements. Such had always served him best anyway, and it was especially true here. Against the claws and tusks of gnarled shimmering ape-like things, the metal padding was little better than parchment. The last to die had done so minutes ago, and not from any beast's talons. Rather, his foot had sunk in a deep spot as they'd slogged through the bog, he'd fallen, and his heavy metal outfit had filled up. By the time the others got his head above water, he'd drunk up the bog beyond belching it out.

"I was trying to figure out what I'm hearing," said the

man called Yeorg, "and where it's coming from. So be quiet, before it sneaks up and kills us."

Yeorg caught himself marveling at the youthful strength and coordination, the sharpness of mind and senses and fighting instincts, as they'd returned to him since... *returned?* Oh, but that was beyond odd! He was the youngest chosen for the quest, barely more than a squire when they'd struck out. Where had it come from, then, that moment's notion of himself as a broken knight, only a few years older yet already crippled and bitter? He'd even felt an impression of the land in which that other self lived. But these impressions faded. The fumes rising from this wicked moon-ruled swampland were all he had room for...all he *wanted*, for he'd never known such revelry at the surge of life through his veins!

His companions hated the smell here, said it was too much like the scorched stench that had choked the countryside back home in the wake of the obsidian beasts. Yeorg had forgotten the smells of his homeland, before or after the dragons.

A shriek ripped at his ears and he spun, nearly losing footing in the mud. The knight in the rear had barely reached the shore when a long reptilian head shot out of the water, its fanged frothing jaws clamping on his midsection. With failing strength, the man twisted, his sword lashing about and swooping up and down, so he chopped out one of the creature's eyes. The quivering, vice-like jaws only tightened. The shrieks grew louder, more hopeless and agonized, mingled with crunching, tearing metal. Yeorg came in a running slide, downhill through the mud, but the other knight reached the beast first, lifting and dropping a heavy blade on the base of the long neck. The edge turned against tough scales. A sinewy, reptilian arm snapped like a whip from beneath the muck and smashed the man in the face. The man's head rolled and thumped inside his helmet like soggy cabbage in a cooking pot. A sheet of blood flooded darkly over his gorget and painted his mailed chest. The body fell and slid beneath the swamp.

Yeorg went straight for his still-shrieking companion, his own sword lashing free. His heavy blade swung, so the knight's head spun away and splashed somewhere. The body sagged in the creature's jaws. The creature shifted its bulk irritably, sank beneath the muddy water, and swam away with the headless knight still in its mouth.

Shaking and snarling, Yeorg scrambled up towards the light that spilled over the hill. He'd been wary of water monsters while crossing, but the one that had attacked hadn't made the noise that had alarmed him moments ago. That sound was further off, on land. It would be closer now, drawn by the dying shrieks. Stealth would do no more good, and Yeorg was on poor footing for a fight. A growl sounded to his left. He didn't pause. The hulking blue mass barreled along the hilltop, closing in. Yeorg planted his feet as best he could in the muddy slope and pointed his sword at the ground. When the thing charged, he would lift his blade and skewer it. From there, its bulk would probably crush him, if a dying swipe of its claws didn't catch him first. It would be a better death than the water monster had given the other two knights.

The thing came on all fours, its narrow, yellow, horridly human eyes meeting Yeorg's in sentient hatred. Holding its onrushing gaze, he lifted his blade. Still several yards away, the creature spasmed. Its eyes rolled up into its skull and its body pitched up on its hind legs. Its back arched and its huge gut heaved and jiggled like a giant pustule sack. It crashed on its side and slid through the muck towards Yeorg. He sprang aside, splashed in the mud, and slid down the slope alongside the dead beast. From the back of the monster's neck, there stuck the oddly curved handle of a small knife, straight through the spine.

Yeorg caught a protruding root, pulled himself up, and sheathed his sword. A slim black shape slid past him down the slope on strongly balanced legs. Yeorg watched the figure pluck the knife from the wound, just before the corpse's bulk slid into the mire. A man, Yeorg noted with astonishment, though clearly better accustomed to this environment than any knight. Yeorg reached level ground. The other man darted over in half the time. His clothes were uniformly black, strangely woven, tight around a slim, dynamic frame. His hair was dark and closely clipped like a Roman, though his bone-pale features were purely of the Isles. His green eyes sparkled like sharp emeralds, and a straight livid scar ran from his right temple to his jawline. When he pressed the back of the small blade with his thumb, it *actually folded forward into the handle.* He slipped it into a pocket sewn into the hip of his strange black britches, then addressed Yeorg:

"Hawkins? How'd you get here? Wouldn't've thought you the sort."

The voice was rough but crisp, in an accent that reminded Yeorg of his homeland's lower peasantry. The words were clearly rooted in the same language, yet so different in nuance and pronunciation that it might as well have been a foreign tongue. Here, though, in this unreal world, Yeorg found he understood perfectly, as with some previously unknown part of his mind.

"Who's Hawkins?" said Yeorg. "Where did you come from?"

"Ah. Well, you see, Inspector, I paid a call to an old mate in Limehouse, fell back to an old habit for the evening, and all this was the vision I slipped into. I suppose now I know why it's called *chasing the dragon.*"

"What do you know of dragons?"

The man ignored the question and shrugged. "Likely I'll eventually wake from it to find I've lost only a few hours, though the longer it seems to last, the truer it all feels. So either you've been on my mind so much lately that you've manifested in that sodden old garb – no funny notions, now; we're just mates – or I truly *have* taken a holiday in some bygone age, and this here stands the shape you wore back then."

"What are you blathering about, you deranged ruffian?"

The man gave a growling laugh. "Aye, that's ol' Hawkins, sure enough, whatever age this is...though younger, I dare say. Either way, we're murdering precious time. Come on, then."

"What?" Yeorg asked. "Where?"

The man pointed uphill and darted back up the ridge. Yeorg hurried up after him, on heavier, shakier legs. He'd been so caught up in the heaving, straining frenzy of battle, he'd nearly forgotten the goal for which he fought...a goal that now awaited within reach.

At the top of the ridge, they passed between twisting black trees, then paused and gazed outward. The moon was nearly full, illuminating a smooth bare field that spread for miles around, speckled in towering egg-like huts. At the center of the field, there arose the largest hut, with light spilling through a sloping triangular doorway. Peering harder, Yeorg saw that all the shapes had such entry points, though no light came from within the others.

Yeorg turned back to the strange, scarred, green-eyed man. "Is that the way to the dragon council? Do you come from them?"

"Heh. That down there *is* the dragon council, mate. Now hurry along. What in the bleeding hell were you doing off the path, anyhow?"

"Our captain, the fool, he –"

"Never mind. Tell me as we go, if you feel the need."

With that, the green-eyed man darted nimbly down into the field. As Yeorg followed, it sank in: he was the last. *That's not how it's supposed to be,* something in him cried. *The dragon council sent for a* company *of knights. It was a* company *they wished to arm and send back, so that we may hunt the demon king's dragons together.*

All this was useless lamentation, yet something in his consciousness felt misled, as though he'd been shown fate's path, and this wasn't what he'd seen. Such delusions were the fatal folly of fools, so Yeorg pushed it from his mind. His strange guide claimed outright to be from another time, to know Yeorg there as someone named *Hawkins* or *Inspector*. Strange names. Clearly the man was no soldier, yet he spoke to Yeorg in the unmistakable way of a close comrade of many battles. Yet Yeorg felt no link between this man and the other incarnation he'd sensed earlier, as though the connections lay in two separate future ages.

No matter. His duty lay at hand. He followed the friendly madman across the field towards the central hut, casting glances everywhere. The hut-like structures were far larger and more intricate than they'd appeared from afar. Beneath the fattening moon, the central dome loomed like a monolith. A tight cleft ran down the center between glistening emerald shingles, splitting into the glowing doorway. The full moon came to rest directly overhead. No sun could have illuminated the world brighter.

The green-eyed man stepped aside. "After you, Inspector."

Once Yeorg stepped within the glowing chamber, he sensed that the very air he breathed in here was made of some pulsing, utterly alien life, emanating inward from the walls. With each breath, it mingled deeper with his own flesh, 'til he felt like something alien unto himself. The rear wall swelled inward bulbously, behind a clay altar that rose from the earth. Atop the altar, there lay a long sword, the narrow blade bright as pearl, but with a greenish tinge. Yeorg wanted to approach for a closer look, but he felt frozen in place. From the base of the bulging wall, there extended a pair of lean, taloned feet. Yeorg's eyes trailed up along the bulge, to the top of the enclosure. At the end of a snaky neck, an enormous reptilian head bobbed downward. Yeorg thought of the water monster at first, but the difference between this creature and that was greater than between a wise old warrior poet from an outland savage. As the dragon chief's unreadable eyes looked knowingly into Yeorg's, he realized the walls around him were its wings, their tips planted deep within the soil.

"Forgive me that I come alone, great beast," said Yeorg. "Only I survived the journey..."

The dragon responded with a thought, one Yeorg heard within his head as though from his own mind. *I know already what has transpired in my land. I would not have it otherwise. You will note, I present only* one *sacred blade of myself.*

"But the party...The call was sent for *seven —*"

And you were not deceived, save by your own assumptions.

Yeorg thought of the spindly, dancing, golden-haired elf that had come before the faded, tattered court, told the beleaguered gathering of kings and queens and chieftains of the quest that must be undertaken, led the chosen knights to the edge of this moon-ruled land. They had all expected the elf to stay with them in the stone circle they had laid, to lead them from there to the dragon chief. But the elf had merely instructed them not to stray from the path, then sprang away and vanished into the alien woodland before they could catch up.

You begin to understand, Yeorg. Of the knights of your lands, there were seven I sensed out who might *wage my crusade against my fallen children in your lands...but only one who would brave* my *lands successfully.*

"Why such waste? They were fine men, men you might have used! Why rely on only one to..."

Among those who might *prove worthy, rarer still is he who* does. *The flame-headed upstart has sent some of those he has corrupted to scorch your land, so that he may recreate it as his own. From there, he would build new legions to bring back here, against all dragonkin. My own strength must remain in my land, against the flame-headed one, but the threats he sows elsewhere must be stamped out. Such primitive realms would be ill suited to meet his threat, so I may spare only a little of my essence to a single warrior from such a realm, with my blessing to lead his own kin against mine. But before I trust one with such responsibility...*

"...Before being so entrusted, the warrior must make himself one with the lands and the chief for whom he now acts." The words came from Yeorg, but he couldn't tell if it was himself drawing the conclusion, or if the dragon chief spoke through him, to root the revelation irrevocably in his heart. He listened for more words. None came.

The green-eyed man's hand touched Yeorg's shoulder. "There you are then, mate. Now take up your gift and be on your way home. You've years of work ahead of you, back there."

Yeorg stared with a moment's desperation, overwhelmed as the implications sank in. Finally, he walked to the altar and reached for the sword. The handle and guard were carved from iron-hard bone, wrapped in blue-tinged hide. The pommel was carved, he noted, in the likeness of the dragon chief's own head. Yeorg's fingers fitted so naturally around the handle that he could no longer imagine wielding any other blade, ever again. He would return to the land of his birth, continue his service there, but never again to that land's kings or gods. 'Til the day he was slain, then through all other lives to follow, Yeorg would be a warrior for the dragon chief beneath the unsleeping moon. With his free hand, he drew the sword he'd come wearing and cast it aside forever.

As he turned to go, the green-eyed man caught his shoulder again. "One more thing, mate."

Yeorg's brows lifted.

"That blade, I hammered it out myself, at his instruction."

"Fine craftsmanship," Yeorg remarked.

"Plucked the choicest scales from his own hide, he did,

melted 'em together with that fiery breath of his, before handing them over to me. But you know, it ain't finished yet, not for what it needs doing. It don't have a *taste*, see, for what it's made to slay."

"A taste?"

"Them damned beasts you go to rid your world of...*my* world too, though my days on its soil lie countless ages ahead. I expect you'll still be doing the good work with that blade, long after that age has come and gone. But the damned beasts...they come from him, are his flesh and blood at the core, no matter what they've been twisted into."

"What am I to do?"

The man pointed his green eyes at the blade's tip, then nodded to the swell of the dragon chief's belly. "So give it your best poke. He's a tough old beast, and he knows it's what you must do, so he won't begrudge you it, much."

The words sank in, and still Yeorg looked back and forth. Finally, with one great surge of will, he sprang forward, leaping over the altar and letting out a furious cry that echoed through the enclosure. His sword drove into the dragon chief's hide, and the spirit of the dragon lands surged through the metal, galvanizing Yeorg, even as the dragon chief's blood spilled out over him. It covered his clothes and his flesh beneath, bathing him, cleansing him of the filth of his journey. It scalded him, hotter than flame, obliterating all he had been, filling him with whom he would ever more be.

His eyes snapped open and he bolted upright, sliding sideways off the couch and crashing onto the wooden floor. His old injuries woke up and shrieked.

Nick pulled himself up, coughing and blinking. The

apartment was choked with the smoke of Dragon's Blood incense.

By next Friday, Nick hadn't made much progress on the comic. His sketchbook was full of swords and dragons, and he was in enough pain that more and more people asked what was wrong. He should go home, smoke it off, draw it off, sleep it off, but he found himself at The Old French Bastard again. More lights glowed this time, but the place was still infuriatingly dim. Sandalwood incense burned in the long brass holder.

"Hello again, young friend," said the old man with that damn smile of his. "Has the week been taxing?"

"Got any more Dragon's Blood?"

Before the old man could answer, Nick glanced at the wall covered in ancient weapons. He froze and stared. Something new hung there today...an ancient long-sword with a handle wrapped in dark, blue-tinged leather. In the dim light, the blade gleamed like pearl with a hint of a green shimmer. Nick moved forward and lifted it from the wall. He could already tell, this was no fantasy-replica wall-hanger. His fingers found the proper grip instinctively. The sweet, cleansing flame of the dragon chief's blood flowed out of it, up through his arms, burning away the agony of his old wounds forever. In its place, there blazed a new clarity and vigor. Nick smelled fire and blood, and the churning pulp of the swamp.

He turned to the old guy and asked, "How much for this?"

Paulie, Ronnie, and Michelle

Hi Paulie,

I found out you're living in Meredith Falls now. Wow, that's something, you here in Vermont! I'm living down in Sturgeon. What do you know, right? My friend Carol was down here last week. She showed me pictures she took at the MF Ren Fair. I spotted you in the background in a couple of them. How random is that? I pointed to you and asked if she knew who you were. You know Carol Beckett, right? Facebook says you do. That's how I got your e-mail address. So here I am, typing this to you at four in the morning. I sent you a friend-request on Facebook. I hope you remember me.

Wow, fighting in a suit of armor in the Renaissance Fair, huh? Cool! You have longer hair than I remember, but no way could I miss that nose and those eyebrows. You look good in that heavy metal, baby! That's a real medieval suit of armor, right? Like a regular Knight in Shining Armor. It reminds me of when we lived in that old big creepy house in New Orleans back in the day, with the crazy old hippie. What was his name? Charlie, right? Yeah, you, me, Ervin and Lenny. Lenny's dead now. I don't know if you knew. We got together, Lenny and me, not long after everything fell apart in that house, but before he died. No one knows where Ervin is anymore. Someone said he's on the run from the law. It seems like everyone we used to know is either dead or missing.

Anyway, yeah, I saw those new pictures of you, in armor with a sword and shield. I thought of when my dad showed up with a trunk of my old junk from my family's place. You got along with my dad when he visited. I think he liked you because you were the most normal out of all of us, or acted like it. I don't know what he told you. I know he acted like he was just being a good dad, bringing his grown-up baby girl a trunk of stuff for her new place. It was actually his final step in disowning me, getting rid of all that old "satanic crap along with me." A lot of that old family junk was actually old artifacts that used to belong to my great-great-grandmother on my mom's side. She was a witch in New Orleans too, and now I was a witch in New Orleans, doing Tarot readings in Jackson Square. I haven't been into that practice in years. I still haven't talked to my dad again, though.

There were those two real-metal wall-hanger swords in that chest, too, with the sharpened tips. You and Ervin picked them up and I know you guys were just playing with them, but you started fencing with them in the living room. You went all up and down the stairs, and I really thought you guys were gonna hurt each other! I know, I still laughed about it a lot. Crazy times, man! Do you even remember that? You guys must have been pretty fried that morning. Now look at you. I guess some things never change, ha ha.

I'm getting married next month. Anyone special in your life these days? I hope so. You sure deserve someone special. You're a great guy. My man Ronnie plays a blues guitar every Friday night at the local pool-hall here in

Sturgeon. You should come down here and visit sometime. I'd love it if you can come to the wedding. I hear you work as a chef in one of the nicest restaurants in town. Woo-hoo, good for you! I always knew you were going places. Ronnie's a great guy. You two would get along. He does martial arts at the local dojo every week. He really likes Japanese swords and knife-throwing. He's very good at knife-throwing.

Paulie, I have a confession to make. When we lived in New Orleans together, I told you I was an ex-junkie. I was still using, though. I started back on it about halfway through the time we were together. I hid it from you. I'm so sorry I lied the whole time. I understand if you don't want to talk to me now! Maybe you always knew. You know how good I was at keeping secrets, though. No one but you in that house, or in that town, even knew about my daughter. I shared things with you that I never shared with anyone else. I'm not lying about that. There were things I didn't even know about myself until I told you. That's stayed with me. It will always mean so much. It's why part of me will always love you like back then.

I'm not a mess like that anymore. I'm allowed to talk with my daughter on the phone now, twice a week. She's a teenager now. How many years has it been?

There's a lot of other bad stuff I still haven't confessed, because I haven't worked up the guts yet. I promise I'll tell you the truth, though. I owe you that much, more than you know.

I really hope you're not mad that I hooked up with Lenny after I left you. Like I said, we stayed with his folks in Maine for a while. They kicked us out when they found out about our habit and how I was the one who got him into it. We wound up down in Sturgeon, Vermont, staying with people he knew, trying to start over. That didn't go well either. His habit got worse than mine. After it finally killed him, I got worse. A lot worse. I fell in with bad people and did what I had to do to get my fix. I went through every kind of hell you can imagine and worse, and I know you don't have to imagine a lot. You told me some about prison. I'm sorry if it hurts for me to mention that, but yeah. I was in the Brattleboro Retreat for a while. That's where I met Ronnie.

Yeah, I know, right? I met my future husband in the psych ward! It's not like that, though, really. He just went through a bad patch and checked himself in there to clear it up. We first met in the cafeteria, under orderly supervision. A while after we both got out, we met up and recognized each other by chance. We talked, one thing led to another, and all that. He has a history of substance abuse too, so we connected in that way.

Before we met in the Retreat, he tried a lot of different ways to conquer his own inner demons. All sorts of spirituality, meditation, you know, every manifestation you can think of, the whole *higher power* thing. When he got out of the Retreat, he got back into his martial arts, I mean got really, super-hard-core into it, all the mind-power ancient philosophy and everything.

Speaking of the whole mind-power thing, before he checked into the Retreat, Ronnie tried conquering his addictions with a lot of mysticism and spiritual woowoo. I mean way weirder, trippier stuff than that New Orleans witchcraft you remember me being into. I don't know what you believe about that kind of thing, but he sure is big on it. There were some things he learned in that phase of his life that stuck with him.

Ronnie's dojo is in this crappy, torn-up, cracked-pavement little riverside strip-mall. There's not much there besides the dojo, and nothing else seems to stay open in that location for long. For a few weeks, though, a while ago, there was this great antique shop. Just one week it was there, and a few weeks later, gone. This weird little old man ran the place, with a funny glassy eye and huge eyebrows. Something Dodson, I think his name was. It was such a cool, interesting little shop while it was there, though. You would have loved it. Ronnie and I went in there and browsed a few times after he got out of class. The front glass was lined in all these black, purple and gold tapestries, around a window display full of tribal sculptures, on a bed of shiny polished pebbles. Whenever you went inside, it looked so dark at first, and everything was so still, you'd think it was closed and left unlocked by accident, 'til the old guy said something to you and you realized he'd been standing there the whole time.

There was always some heady, musky incense burning that I didn't recognize. I kept meaning to ask the old guy what it was, but whenever I stepped inside, just everything about the whole atmosphere would overwhelm me so I'd forget, like I'd really just stepped out of one world into another.

Ronnie and I didn't have the money for most of the really cool stuff we really liked in there, but the old guy saw us eyeing this really neat full-length Victorian mirror, the kind on a spinning gilded rotator thingy, only the frame of this one is engraved with a lot of ancient glyphs and symbols from ancient cultures and forgotten cults. You know, like the ones you showed me pictures of, from all those old weird books you used to collect in the back-alley used book stores in New Orleans. Anyway, the old guy cut us a sweet deal, so we brought that mirror home. Next time we went back to the strip-mall, we found the shop gone, just gone. The store space was totally bare and deserted. Weird, huh? At least that mirror has a nice home in this one bare-stone corner of our apartment. We use the back area as both an art studio and Ronnie's ritual space.

Ronnie has some nightly meditation and spell-work rituals I think you'd really find fascinating. He likes to light several colors of candles, arrange them just so around the sacred area, sit Indian-style in front of that mirror, meditate, and gaze off into the flames. I don't know if he would want me telling you, having not met you and all, but I feel like I should. I feel like you have a right to know.

I've watched him at it. He's invited me into the sacred circle with him. I've seen what happens. I've felt what happens. When you look into that mirror at those times, you see other worlds on the other side. Not like *totally different* worlds. It's still our room and our place on the other side, but the more you look, the more you notice what's different, little things that add up so there's no question about it. You're looking at another universe. More than one, in fact. I sit at Ronnie's side in the candlelight, look through those mirrors, and those other worlds look back at us. When we keep the blinds on the window open, and start at the right hour of dusk, there really is a totally different scene outside. There's none of the usual surrounding houses or cars or trees, but the jungle of another kingdom, the Kingdom of the Flame King.

I reminded you of that old trunk my dad brought me in New Orleans. I still have some of the stuff from it, mostly the kind of artifacts and curious lore that used to belong to my great-great grandmother, same kind of stuff you might find in Mister Dodson's shop. The more I make sense of it, the more I think she wasn't the kind of witch I tried to be back in the day. She was something completely different, more like what I'm becoming now. I think now, maybe Dad knew more about all that than he ever said. Maybe that's really why he was so eager to get rid of both me and all that old stuff. I wouldn't blame him. He wouldn't have lasted long in the world the Flame King's going to let Ronnie and me into.

One of the things I still have from that old trunk is this little brass stand, sort of like a candle-holder, except it's molded to hold a certain special smooth, marble-like, egg-shaped stone. You remember the stone I mean. That was in the trunk too. It looked purple or blue or some weird spectral combination of the two, depending what light you held it in. I know you know the one, because I remember how you used to sit at the kitchen table and just stare at it for hours, so fascinated. Do you remember how I used to sit there and look at it with you?

Neither of us could figure out where it came from, even when we tried doing research into what kind of stone it was. It belonged in that little brass stand in the windowsill, but now I can't find it. Except when I see that stand through the mirror, the stone's there. Always, until we look away from the mirror, back at this world, and the holder is still empty.

Here's how it is, Paulie. Through the window, in the mirror, the Flame King's eyes blaze in at us during the Ritual Hour. The Flame King tells us that once we have the stone back in this world, and set it in its proper place, the barrier will dissolve between us, and we'll be allowed to step fully into the world of the Flame King, on the other side of the mirror, where we'll be rewarded for finding him. I ask the Flame King where the stone is. He shows me your face.

So I know you have it. You must have kept it, from the trunk, back then. The more I think about it, the more it makes sense. Except it doesn't need to make sense. It's just plain fact. The Flame King told me. He told Ronnie, too. He showed Ronnie your face. We need that stone back from you, like now.

Paulie, I told you I had other things to confess too you. I had to work myself up to this, though. I talked to Carol about you, and she found your home address for me. I started writing you this letter planning to print it out, send it to you in the mail the old fashioned way. But Ronnie's on his way to your place now, and he's not going to leave until he gets the stone back from you. So I hope you're awake and reading this e-mail, because Ronnie will be there soon. He'll get in, one way or another. He won't leave until he finds what he came to find. I hope you're civil with him. I know you can handle yourself, but trust me, honey, you don't know Ronnie.

I hope we can talk and catch up soon.
Love,
Michelle

Lambs of Slaughter in Blue and Gold

I've followed her for days, and I've almost gotten used to *how much this hurts!* It hurts less at night, but she sleeps too much then. She never used to. Often that was because of me, last time, when we both stood at the crossroads, the ones she's headed back to now.

If I tried, I could keep her awake. She'd deserve it, right? She's the one who makes it hurt. But I always drift behind her, and she never senses me. So why do I know how blue her eyes are, that that's where this infernally tranquil sea floods out of? If I stepped in front of her, would she see me with her eyes now, or her eyes from back then? I only get to look at her face when she sleeps. She looks almost exactly the same! Even with the lights off, I can see that. At those times, I can almost relax, almost forget the shredding agony her blue glow locks me in when she's awake.

Now she walks around town, smells the summer smells of pollen, thistles, and fresh-cut grass. I smell it with her, scorching my brimstone nostrils. She drops by the same places where things happened. She hangs out with her friends, drinking and smoking up and playing the guitar she's learning, telling ghost stories in the woods and graveyards and the abandoned sawmill lot, all the same spots we used to go.

No one tells the *best* ghost stories anymore, the ones I was there for, even when they sit on the same spots where things happened. Maybe I should do something about that. You can't say I'm not in the unique position to do so. I have other things on my mind, though. She makes out with boys in the same spots in the woods where we used to make love, next to the railroad tracks or that sandy spot by the river. The town's full of such places, places where things happened, *and she never notices!*

She hangs out in a coffee shop that used to be a speakeasy, back when we were both young and alive and together. We weren't much older than she is now, but we got in one night, dressed in fancy hand-me-downs to look the best we could like the gangsters and dames we'd seen in the pictures.

By then, she was already used to drinking. I wasn't. She thought it was so cute how I tried to act tough, pretended to hold my liquor better than I did, how I got snappy when she noticed.

It was one of *them* who ran that speakeasy. He wore a wide-brimmed hat like a preacher, but otherwise looked like the pinstriped gangster you'd expect to run a place like that. When he took an interest in us, we were scared out of our minds at first. We thought he knew we were too young, that he'd kick us out, tell our folks. Which I have to admit is pretty silly, considering the kind of place it was to begin with, but you know how kids are. The truth was, he'd noticed what we'd only faintly started to notice in ourselves. He bought us drinks and said things that made us sure he was off his rocker. By the end of that night, though, we understood plenty. He showed us things going on in that speakeasy that no one else saw. Or if they did, they mistook it for odd shapes the cigarette smoke made in the air. He got us plenty drunk, too.

She managed to sneak into her house that night, to pass out like a good girl. I woke up in the speakeasy's basement. My pa beat me plenty when I staggered home with an obvious hangover, but I didn't mind so much anymore. I just grinned through it, which made him think I'd gone crazy so he beat me worse. Now I understood that the pain was just weakness being chased out of my body, letting in strength I'd need for the new world my eyes had been opened to...a world of power we'd build right under the noses of this silly little town.

Now she drifts through it all, sleepy and sad, not quite sure about what...through the sea that bleeds out through the air around her, from her clear blue eyes. It's the soft blue that hurts so much. After the last time, I awoke in the scorching blackness that's almost red, a constant blaze that feels wonderful to me because I'm part of it. Bit by bit, it's replaced everything but my memories. As I've learned to work this new ephemeral matter, I've mastered it. I rule it, along with everything it touches in the world it bleeds out into. My fingertips are needles, and my bones are sharpened with sword edges. In the realms I travel, I flex and flail my razor limbs, cutting to ribbons anything stupid enough to come against me. I suck in those bloody ribbons like spaghetti and grow ever stronger. But my blades can't touch the blue that bleeds from her eyes, mingling with the reddish gold that wafts off her silky hair. Now I'm trapped in it, following her until she wakes up...to me, to everything she doesn't notice yet.

Most of the others who were involved, they're still around. No one knows they're the ones really pulling the strings around here. They're all old men and women now, older than most folks live, and they'll live to be a lot older. Or at least they plan to. She's seen them, met them, and she doesn't recognize them, but I do. I pick through her memories while she dreams. Since I showed back up, she hasn't happened to bump into any of them again. They're not folks she'd think to look for, folks she knows well or anything...just another cluster of faces you'll get used to seeing around a small town and never think anything of.

She kisses her mom goodbye and goes to her summer job. Her mom's broke as hell, can barely feed her two daughters, but she decided to have another baby with one of her here-and-gone boyfriends – yeah, *decided to*, worked on it 'til she missed a period and cooed at the top of her lungs with joy. She was even happier when it turned out to be her first boy, even when the brat popped out with fetal alcohol syndrome. Their house is on lines that have been knotted up and ruptured in places, letting astral fumes into the brains of the people who live there, to encourage that kind of thinking. *They* rewired the town like that, decided who got rich and who stayed poor and stupid, the better to support what they've built, the one they're gearing up to expand.

Maybe they *did* arrange it for her to be reborn there – would be a smart move – but I don't think they're powerful enough yet to direct which souls are reborn where. If they were, they'd probably have pulled me back as her addled little brother. Wouldn't that be a kick in the crotch...if I hadn't found my way to this scorching blackness first. Funny thing is, they're the ones who opened that door for me, or rather showed me the door so I could open it. I'll thank them properly soon, with some help from her.

She works in a junk shop that used to be someone's house. We used to have meetings in that house, she and I and *them*. The middle-aged guy who runs the place now doesn't have anything to do with them, is blind as everyone else, but he's an asshole, and I don't like seeing her do what he tells her. I could set maggots writhing in his brain, knock him off his high horse, make him hop and roll around like a monkey on acid so she could laugh at him...if she wasn't ripping me apart and washing everything I'm made of away, over and over again, in that hellishly gentle blue of hers. But it's slow today in the junk shop, and the boss isn't around. The boy she made out with last night in the woods slips in like he's not supposed to be there, like the boss'll kick his ass if he catches him there, and he creeps up to her like the sheepish pissant he is. She smiles and kisses him. He asks if he can see her tonight, then tries to slip out, says he doesn't want to loiter around and get her in trouble, but she tugs him back and kisses him again.

Something gurgles and pops in me, something of the fire she's stolen trying to shoot back through me. For an instant, I'm almost myself again...long enough to slide my arm past her slender soft waist and sink my claw right into this little pissant's guts and *twist*. He doubles up and backs away. I hold onto his guts. He looks like he'll puke all over the place, and he turns away so it won't splatter on her. With my claws still in him, the motion only hurts him worse. She asks him what's wrong. I imagine how scared her blue eyes must look. Then I feel how close my razor arm is to her, between her arm and her waist. I remember being able to caress her, wish I could now without cutting her. It's just enough for her peaceful blue sea to drown me again. I jerk back.

The young man straightens himself out, gleaming with fresh sweat. "Sorry," he quavers. "I should go home. I don't feel so good."

Once he's gone, she says, "Why'd you do that?"

I try to pulse with my own infernal matter, but it's not there anymore. I'm lost in her sleepy blue peace again. It burns worse than ever. "What?" I manage. "You know I'm here?"

"Of course. I've noticed since you showed up. I just wondered why you wouldn't talk to me. Why are you so pissed off all the time? Is it 'cause you're in so much pain?"

"Little bitch, it's you! How stupid can you be? You're what's causing the pain, holding me prisoner." As if in retaliation, the blue sea beats and stabs through me, tearing me apart so maybe, this time, there won't be anything left by the time she's done with me. I just tried to say *I love you* and those were the words that came out instead.

"No," she says, "I'm not. Why do you say it like I'd think it was the other way around? You haven't tried to hurt me. I've sort of wondered why not, to be honest, angry and hurting and scared like you always are. You haven't tried to hurt anyone 'til you attacked Jerry just now."

I manage a hoarse laugh, made of razors that cut up my throat from the inside. "Don't worry about him. He's so dull, I'd have to strike a *lot* harder to do real damage. That's why it's so much more *rewarding* when the dullards feel the attacks and actually get some halfwit idea of what's happening to them...when I get through their thick skulls and rip their brains apart. But I can't anymore, because you won't let me."

"I'm not stopping you."

"Yes you are, and you damn well know it! Quit fucking with my mind!"

"So why are you even latching onto me? There are plenty of mean folks around here who'd be glad to let you hurt whoever you wanted. You could latch onto some violent drunk in a bar, cause all kinds of bad stuff to happen, I'll bet."

How did I miss that she's this *awake?* How much *does* she know? "I haven't *latched onto you!* It was *you* who lured *me* back, trapped me in this shmoopy blue glue always farting out around you!"

"*Shmoopy's* a funny word."

"Damn you, *how can you not know?*" Again, there's me trying to say it: *Because I love you.* Is it her matter the words keep getting lost in, or mine? It's hard enough to think, in this blue scorch she creates. If she could just wash away my memories, it wouldn't hurt anymore. But I *can't* forget. I can't be free 'til I've brought her to her true awakening.

"Know what?" she says

"I can't believe you don't remember." What would happen to me if she turned and looked at me right now? I don't want to know, yet the need boils hotter and hotter, to *tell her to look,* say *Turn around, bright eyes* and see how long I'd last in that horrid ecstasy.

"Remember what?" Those two words alone are almost enough to kill me, again.

"How can you be as *awake* as you are and still wander around like a little idiot, so damn blissfully ignorant of everything going on around you?"

"Yeah, like what? Other than you, I mean."

By now, she's pissed me off enough to give me more strength than I thought I could muster, caught here in her nasty drowning tranquility. I could tell her about it so she'd believe me, remind her who we used to be together, remind her of *them* so she'd know their faces before spotting them again, know what they did, how they're slowly killing her and everyone she loves.

Instead I just say, "Oh, don't worry. You'll find out soon enough."

She shrugs, says "Fine," then goes through the junk shop, straightening the clothes racks and shelves. Some customers come in and she sees to them.

We don't speak to each other for the rest of her shift. We still don't when she gets off work. She goes to that coffee shop she likes so much, talks to people she knows there, then takes out a science fiction novel she's been reading and sits for an hour or so sipping coffee. Like she's forgotten I'm there, like we never talked in the junk shop after I attacked her little pissant boyfriend, and the world's still the same sleepy mundane place its always been. She's too comfortable here for such things to matter. The weird part is, the longer we're here, the more I feel like I could be too. As the hours pass, it hurts less and less. I almost remember how it felt, when this was a speakeasy and we were here together, before the owner approached us. Those last moments when we were nothing but a couple of crazy kids in love breaking the rules, unable to imagine what could be more exciting, how we could possibly feel more alive.

When it's almost closing time, the owner comes in and lets the kid working the counter go home early. Then the owner's turned the Open sign to Closed. She hasn't noticed because she's lost in her book. All the customers have filtered out but her.

The owner's an old man. He's owned this place since before it was a coffee shop. Now he dresses like an old hippie, but he still wears that wide-brimmed preacher hat...pulling the town's strings, keeping his own people rich or at least comfortable, keeping everyone else poor and stupid and slowly dying, without them even noticing it's him. All the while, he masks himself as just a little old small business owner, dressing dirt poor for his cover, when he's not out with the others or up living in one of those big fancy houses on the edge of town, with servants and everything. Some of the servants these folks keep are even human. Sometimes they get to leave those big, fancy houses for a while. The rest of the time, even I don't envy them.

I can't tell if he recognizes her, except as one of the folks he's kept low. He *should* recognize her. He should sense me with her. We're the ones he led in, so we could be the lambs of slaughter that opened the doors to the forces that showed him how to do what he does to the people now.

I remember the night he led us out to the old sawmill where the ritual would be held. We thought we'd merge with what we'd draw forth together, so we could work with him to make things *better* for everyone. We stripped naked and stood before him and the others, as the bonfire blazed and he spoke the words of the ritual. I remember how we looked at each other lovingly. We were so scared, but our eyes gave each other strength because we weren't scared of what we should have been. We still thought we were about to be knighted with the ceremonial knife he drew. I should have thought about how that knife was shaped, the upper edge serrated and split in two down the center, to catch the sacrificial blood. She never saw it coming. It should have all snapped into place in my brain, right as he moved to knight her first. I should have stopped it. Instead I heard what sounded like a hiccup, then I turned in time to see the blade slide out of her chest, loosing a dark spout into the air, straight from her heart. All I could do was stare like an idiot, destroyed already by the sight of her death, right before the blade licked into my own heart.

As I slumped to the earth and faded out, I heard *him* bellow the ritual's final words. I felt the doors open as *he'd* planned, and I went through them, passing the forces he drew forth on my way. She went somewhere else and found her way back, so she could call me back for this reckoning without even realizing it.

Now is the time, but she hasn't looked up at him yet. I see the speakeasy this place used to be. I see us sitting and laughing together in it, before he came up. She might be sitting at the same table now. It's the same spot, I realize.

"Excuse me, miss. I'm about to lock up. You can finish your drink first if you like."

"Don't look up at him," I hiss. Why did I just say that? Isn't this what I was champing at the bit for all along?

"Why not?" she says to me.

The old man twitches, confused. "Huh?"

She looks up and sees him. "Oh, I'm sorry, I –" She stops and stares, remembers the knife sliding in and out of her heart...all because I'm here with that memory and others.

Then comes a final pure flare of that sea of blue and gold of hers. By now, it no longer hurts at all, like the scorching blackness I'm made of has been replaced by it. Then it dies. What's left of it flares to full force against me before we finally mix into a murky red that floods the room. Both essences scorch me. I feel them start to scorch her. I try to fight it back, to keep it off her.

No, don't let it touch her! She doesn't need it! Let her live her life! Let her make out with that pissant and any other boys she likes, 'til she grows up and gets out of this evil place and has a better life somewhere else, away from them, away from me, never the wiser.

I try to shout a lie that could save her, something like *Quit playing with this scorching darkness, you stupid ignorant bitch! You're out of your league here! This was once your lot, in a life where I was something that mattered to you, where* you *could have mattered.*

What comes out instead is "I love you."

She doesn't seem to hear, just looks at *him*. He stiffens and sweats, because he sees it all. He knows who she is, and he knows I'm here.

"Uh, actually, on second thought, miss, maybe you'd better gulp that down and go. I really need to close up and get home. I can pour it in a to-go cup if you like."

She sets her drink down and stands up. "No, that's okay. Here, let me help you close up."

"I really shouldn't...I mean..."

She hits some light switches on her way to the big window. All I can do is hover and watch, paralyzed in the smoky red her tranquil blue sea has turned into, just like I planned. I try telling myself I haven't stolen anything from her. Her innocence was just on loan anyway, until I showed up to send it somewhere else, maybe to someone who'd be allowed to keep it, if such people ever actually exist. She pulls the cord so the blinds slide down.

"Actually," he starts saying, "I like to leave those…"

She walks past him to the counter. He's as frozen as I am, and a lot more bewildered. She plucks a carving knife from the counter, still sticky from the coffee cake and other treats it carved for customers not long ago. Before he can do anything, she raises the blade and stabs him right in the heart, like he did me…like he did her. He slumps towards the floor like we did to the ground of the sawmill lot. Her face twists with a rage she's never had a chance to feel before, so she stabs him five more times before he lands. He lies there spurting, then leaking faintly. His neck and chest and shoulders are full of jagged fissures of mangled meat, through his shredded shirt. She settles over him, breathing hard.

Finally she looks at me and says, "I love you too." Then she goes and finds the mop bucket he's prepared.

"This isn't right," I say. "I didn't want this for you. I thought I did, but not now! This should've been your second chance, to *not be part of –*"

"Shut up. If you're not gonna help me clean this up and cover our tracks, then just be quiet." I obey, because I'm as much in her power as I've always been. Except now she knows it. The floating essence around her is still changing. I know all too well what it'll be by the time it settles. "The rest of them are still out there. We'll have to deal with them. We'll get to them in due time. And we'll take what they claimed to offer us then, take charge of things, change things like we always said we would."

Our mingled essence settles towards its proper form. In time, I'll come to love it. For now, I watch her work. I want to hold her like I used to. But she's still so soft, and my

STORY TIME WITH CRAZY UNCLE MATT

bones are all razor-edged, my fingertips stabbing needles.

Dead Men, Dead Dogs,
Tasty Bacon

The rain was picking up, and another half mile stretched through the middle of nowhere, between here and the shack they were squatting in. For now, they sat under the bridge. If the summer rain got so bad that the water rose, they'd have to find other shelter, or just bite the bullet and walk home in it. Right now, here was a pleasant stretch of dry sand and clay to sit on, smooth stone to lean against, and they had beer and smokes. Abe leaned back and picked at his guitar, singing when he felt like it. Sean squatted and leaned forward, looking like a raggedy, unshaved gargoyle with a cigarette in one hand and a growler of local brew in the other. Whenever Abe played something Sean knew, Sean sang along between swigs and puffs.

Will had said he wouldn't come back. Abe and Sean both knew that was bullshit. Or they'd find him back at the shack. Hopefully Abe wouldn't keep saying stupid shit to push Will's buttons. Either way, Sean tried to enjoy the moment's peace.

Sean had hooked up with these guys less than two months ago, shortly before they found the shack. These patterns already felt routine.

Someone's feet padded down the bank alongside the

bridge, too light and nimble to be Will's. Around the corner came a medium sized dog. Sean recognized it and listened pensively for the owner. When the owner didn't follow, he wondered if the old fucker had finally keeled over somewhere. Sean still didn't like the animal. They'd seen the guy around a lot. His even-more-disgusting dog followed him everywhere, sometimes into the bar or the general store, sometimes walking along the roadside. The man was so dark all over that Sean had mistaken him for black at first. Then he realized, no, the guy was actually *purple*...as in the festering purple of deep frostbite. That didn't make sense in the summer, even all the way up in northern Vermont, where the night air still liked to bite you all over if you got caught out in it, alone and homeless, and the less friendly sorts had called dibs on whatever makeshift shelter you could find and weren't willing to share.

The nasty old guy wasn't homeless, though, or even poor. His matted hair was all dark brown patches. The bald parts were crusted in blood like someone had ripped the rest of it out by the roots. He spoke in broken sentences, barely intelligible enough to buy beer. He carried large bills that came out of his pockets covered in sticky lint. His rags looked like they'd started out as high class stuff, and those greasy pockets never ran dry. No one seemed to know who he was, when he'd gotten to town, or where he was staying. Then one day in the bar, someone Sean knew went right up to the guy, wrinkled their nose against the smell, and took a long look. The old rotting bastard didn't seem to notice, but the dog had tensed up and snarled.

"I think it's that old doctor fucker," the observer said, "the one from Rhode Island."

That's right, a few months back, everyone had been talking about some weird coot who'd retired from his practice in Providence and moved up north to do private research or something. No one saw much of him, except when he came into town for groceries or a drink. Maybe his research had involved weird drug experiments, and he'd fucked himself up good. The dog looked like it had been getting some of the juice too. Seeing it now, Sean was glad Abe was sitting between him and it. The animal sniffed its way towards them. Its breaths came in high raspy panting, like hacking out air through gravel.

Abe leaned towards the thing and petted it. The animal looked as happy as any normal dog for the attention. "Hey boy, what you doing here? Where's your master, huh?"

Sean sat back and watched, wondering how Abe could stand the smell. He could barely stand it himself at this distance, so he swigged deep and pulled harder on his cigarette. "Careful, dude. That thing's probably full of every disease I never thought of."

"Nah, he's a good boy. He's just under-fed and under-loved. Ain't that right, boy, yes." The thing licked Abe's hands and face with a long, pink, green-speckled tongue.

"I'm just glad you've got your own damn jug to swig from, that's all I'm sayin'," said Sean.

The animal didn't look diseased, so much as put together from spare parts, most of them past their sell-by date. Its slick, grinning lips never covered its red gums or yellow teeth because there wasn't enough lip for the mouth to close fully. The pale brown eyes bulged from the sunken sockets. Sean kept expecting them to pop out and slide down the sides of its face. At least the tiny nose wasn't dribbling snot everywhere. Rather it was dry and shriveled like a raisin. The snout between the raisin nose and bugged-out eyes was narrow, the furless skin shrink-wrapped around the bones. The patches on its scrawny middle looked more like moss than fur. Its tail swung stiffly like a bare twig in the wind. Sean was afraid the thing would turn and point its ass at him, and he'd see dried shit dangling in clumps like seed-pods beneath that tail.

Abe was still making friends with the freaky, stinky dog when heavy footsteps bounded down the hillside. It sounded too lively to be the thing's owner. In the next moment, Will rounded the corner, his long silky hair wild and wet, a giant grin on his face. His eyes were big and friendly. Whenever Will grinned, it made Sean think of a demented hillbilly. It was the long hair, the beard, the burly build, and the fact that Will actually *was* a demented hillbilly, and a precocious one to boot. Sean thought at first, maybe Will had found that girl he'd been talking about. Then he noticed two tightly stuffed grocery bags under one of Will's thick arms.

Will looked at the dog. Some troubled feelings passed through his face like a heavy cloud. "Hey guys," he said. "Man, I scored big time!"

"With that girl?" said Sean.

Will set the bags down against the stone wall. "Nah, she wasn't home."

Sean noticed a fresh bruise on Will's temple, and he wondered who *had* been home. He didn't ask yet because he didn't want to spoil Will's good mood. Will seemed to have forgotten that he'd gone off because he was pissed at Abe. Sean wasn't going to remind him. Hopefully Abe didn't start stirring the pot again.

"Whatch'a got there, buddy?" Abe looked up from the

dog, which kept licking his hands.

"Groceries, man. I got eggs, bacon, shredded cheddar, some milk, some canned beans, soup, more beer, and a whole carton of cigarettes. We can cook tonight on that ol' wood-burnin' stove back at the place."

"How we supposed to keep the shit refrigerated?" asked Sean.

Will's lips twisted and his eyes sparked with petulant irritation. "In the icebox in the basement. I told you, motherfucker, I got the generator wired up and runnin'."

Fair enough, then. Will was crazy, no doubt about it, but he was an unbelievable fix-it monkey when you needed one. While Abe went to explore the grocery bags, the dog turned and looked uncertainly at Will. Sean saw it from behind. Sure enough, there was all that dried shit dangling beneath that dead twig of a tail, in dusty clumps like a few extra sets of balls.

"How'd you afford all this?" asked Sean.

"Y'know Old Man Zombie Doc, or whoever the fuck he was?"

"You mean the guy this dog belongs to?"

"*Belonged* to. Yeah, that guy. I wondered what happened to the dog. Shit, the thing stinks."

"Yeah, it does." Sean looked again at the fresh bruise on Will's temple.

"Relax, man," said Will. "I didn't kill nobody. Fucker went off into the field on the roadside and just dropped dead there, I guess. Far as I know, he's still lyin' out there in the rain."

"Wow." Abe chuckled nervously. "So the old bastard finally kicked off."

"I guess. Hard to tell. He always seemed like a dead

thing to me. 'Cept he was movin' around before, and he ain't now."

"So what'd you do," asked Abe, still examining the groceries, "go through his pockets?"

"Shit yeah, man. That old bastard was always loaded. I'm just the lucky bastard who found him first."

"And no one saw you?" Sean figured it was best to make sure. Still, he was smiling now too. He was almost excited enough by this fresh fortune to forget the not-so-fresh smell.

"Relax, bitch. Nah, no one saw me." Will crouched and turned his attention to the dog. "Hey there. Damn, boy, you stink like your old dead owner. C'mere."

Will started petting the dog. At first, it seemed to like him well enough. Then it sniffed him over. Its whole face and body language changed, twisting into a bristling snarl, eyes black with hate. Will leapt up with a shout. The snarling mutt sank its yellow teeth into his arm and dangled there thrashing. He jerked it loose, flung it down, and it came at him for more. Before it could bite again, though, he clocked it hard on the side of the head. Sean heard something pop, and he was sure the beast would fall over dead now. Will was one abnormally strong sonofabitch, and it didn't look or sound like he'd held back much. That must have been wishful thinking, though, because the dog wobbled around on its brittle, dry-stalk legs and stayed up. It inched towards Will again, still snarling. He grabbed it by the shriveled snout, held its jaws shut, and shook it 'til it calmed down. Sean swore he heard snapped bones grinding against each other somewhere inside the dog, probably in the neck.

The dog seemed to grow limp in Will's grasp, and

Sean thought, *Okay, it'll finally drop dead when he lets go, for sure this time.* Will let go. The dog sat down at his feet.

"There you go," Will murmured. "See, who's a good boy. That crazy old fucker just wasn't takin' care of him right."

Abe kept chuckling nervously. "He sure got pissed off when he smelled whatever you'd done to the old bastard's corpse, though."

Will glowered at Abe. "I didn't do nothin' to no corpse, asshole." He turned his attention back to the dog. "Yeah, you jus' gotta show 'em who's the dominant animal. Can't blame the dog for wantin' to take on the lion. But you ain't never seen a dog win in a fight against that lion, have you? The lion ain't the fuckin' king of the jungle for nothin'." He patted the dog's head roughly. Sean heard more grinding. The dog seemed to wobble more than before, too.

"How's your arm, Lion-boy?" asked Abe.

"Ain't bad. Got any beer left in them jugs?"

Will hadn't let the dog near his mouth, so Sean picked his jug up and held it out. Will reached down and picked up Abe's, though. He swigged deep, then poured the last of it over the red teeth marks on his wrist.

"Hey," Abe said, "you didn't just waste the last of that, did you?"

"Relax, bitch. I already told you, I got better stuff here."

"So you get the old fucker's wallet?" Sean asked.

"I went through it, but there wasn't much there. He kept his big cash stash in his pockets."

"So how much was left?"

"Don't worry, motherfucker, we're set for a while."

"So you still got the wallet?" Sean asked.

Will grunted, took the wallet from his pocket, and tossed it at Sean. Sean caught it and went through it 'til he found an ID card. "Yep, this is ol' Doc West, all right."

"That his name?" Will was still busy socializing with the dog.

Sean didn't find anything else interesting in the wallet, so he put the ID back and tossed it into the creek. After a while he said, "Hey, y'know, the rain's gettin' pretty heavy. We should get out from under this bridge." He was worried about rising water, but mainly it was an excuse to get out from under here where the dog's stench grew thicker and thicker.

"What are you talking about?" asked Abe. "You wanna get drenched?"

"He's right, dude," said Will. "Look at the creek. It's gettin' bigger. We'll get more soaked if we stay under here. Like drowned or some shit, maybe."

Abe put his guitar back in the case and took one of the grocery bags under his other arm. Sean grabbed the other bag. They got back up to the road, got soaked pretty fast, and tried to walk faster. The dog hobbled after them. Will lagged so it could keep up with him. Sean kept glancing back at the creature with morbid fascination. At least in all this rain, the smell wasn't carrying anymore.

When Sean looked at the animal's hide, he swore he saw bits of those mossy patches sliding off in the rain and splashing on the ground to mix with the rest of the muck. "That dog don't look like he's doin' so good."

"Yeah, you're right." Will scooped the dog up and carried it.

When they reached the shack, Sean said, "You ain't

really gonna bring that thing inside, are you?"

"Man, chill out," said Will. "You don't want him pokin' around in your shit, go shut your door."

"I was more worried about him stinking up the whole place," said Sean.

"Aw, he just smelled like that 'cause that fucked-up doc wasn't takin' care of him. He's had a good bath in the rain, though, ain't you, boy?"

When Will rubbed the dog's head, Sean heard more grinding sounds. The wheezing panting sounded more than ever like a gravel-choked gag. The bugged-out eyes rolled around in their oversized sockets. Sean was more convinced than ever that one or both of those eyes would pop out at any second.

Will set the dog down inside. It rolled out of his arms, flopped on the floor, and looked like it wouldn't get up. After a moment, though, it lurched to its feet and started sniffing everything. Actually, it probably wasn't smelling much of anything anymore, just going through the motions. Now when it moved, Sean thought he could hear its guts sloshing around inside like rotted vegetables in a sack. After setting down the groceries, he took Will's advice and shut his bedroom door. He noticed that Abe did the same. Then they all stripped out of their sopping clothes and put on dry pants. It was chilly in the shack, but it warmed up fast when they got the wood stove going. To Sean's surprise, Will was mostly right about the stink. The thing no longer smelled much like a rotting dog, just a wet one. The shack hadn't exactly smelled like a rose garden to start with. The lack of stench let Sean focus again on the thing's appearance and movements, which freaked him out more than anything else, so he ignored it as much as possible. It didn't try to shake itself dry like any other dog would, just lurched around, dribbling a wet trail everywhere. Abe didn't say anything about it, so Sean wouldn't either. There wasn't anything lying in the open for the thing to ruin, really. Will could clean up after it on his own time.

It was getting dark now. As they cooked, Will washed down his prescription meds with lots of beer. This meant the rest of the evening would be much calmer. Once they all had a good hot meal in them, Abe played Hank Williams on the guitar for a while, drank more than anyone else and passed out early. Will put some scraps on a plate and set it on the floor for the dog. It eventually found its way to the meal, ate it mechanically, then wandered around the room some more. Will picked up Abe's guitar and plucked at it absently, somehow creating what sounded like a real song. Finally he set the guitar aside, found the soaking pants he'd worn earlier, and pulled two greasy lint-covered piles of cash from the pocket. Yeah, actually, it looked like they'd be set for a while.

Will counted and straightened the bills, then leaned his elbow on the table and put his bruised forehead in his palm. "I think I took too many pills, Sean. I think I finally overdosed."

This scene was nothing new. "Man, if you die, and I have to get rid of your corpse, I'm gonna be pissed."

"I'm serious, man. I think I'm really dyin' this time. Don't worry, though. Ain't like I mind much."

"Just take it easy, buddy. Lemme know if you need help gettin' to the couch."

Will downed the last of his beer and popped a fresh one. "Nah, it's cool. Jus', sorry if I don't wake up."

There followed some kind of silence that might be

meaningful. Then Sean glanced to the other side of the room. "Will, I *really* don't think your new buddy there is doin' so hot."

"He ain't gettin' into nothin', dude. Leave him be."

"No, I mean look at it. The head's all lopsided, and its belly keeps sagging lower, like any second, it's gonna give out and those rotted guts are gonna spill out all over the floor."

"You're fuckin' sick, dude, y'know that?"

"I'm just tellin' it like I see it."

"An' you're a sick bastard for seein' it like that, so you'd better back off."

Sean was too drunk himself by now to argue earnestly. "Fair enough." He looked at the bite on Will's arm. It was redder and wider than before. "So how'd you get the bruise on your head?"

"Went to that girl's place. She wasn't home, but her dumbass daddy was. He didn't like me much, tried to get into it with me. You should see what he looks like now."

Not long after that, it became impossible to hold a conversation with Will. The dog wandered over and started sniffing Sean's leg. He shoved it away with his foot, and was glad he'd put his boots back on after changing. The dog fell over on its side. This time it didn't get up, just flopped and dragged itself away like a stroke victim trying to swim.

Sean grabbed one more beer, went and drank it in his room, then passed out. When he woke up the next morning, the whole place smelled like the dog. Out in the kitchen, Will had left the money on the table next to a scribbled note.

Hey Guys,
I don't think I'll wake up. I took too many pills, then I drank too much beer on top of them. I can feel my life slipping away, feel myself slipping into darkness.
Love,
Will
P.S. – Sorry, I ate all the bacon. It was delicious. If you get more, try melting some cheddar cheese over it. It's real tasty like that.

Sean found Will sprawled on his back on the couch. Will's left foot had fallen off the side. The dog had come over and chewed on it for a while, exposing some of the bones. Will shifted around and groaned, eyes fluttering. He didn't seem to notice what the dog had done to his foot. It didn't even bleed much. His skin had taken on a deep, unhealthy discoloration. The dog still lay next to the chewed-up foot. Sean wondered if it had ever managed to stand up, or if it had crawled and flopped its way over to Will's foot like that. Its belly had given out and its guts had gone all over the floor. The insides didn't smell much different from the outside, a little more rotted maybe. Its head lulled farther than ever on its broken neck. One of the eyes had finally popped free and dangled on a drying cord. The animal no longer moved.

Sean went and peeked into Abe's room. Abe didn't look so hot either. Sean remembered the dog licking Abe's face and hands with its green-speckled tongue. Sean shut the door and went back to the table. Will was fumbling for the top of the couch, as if hoping to pull himself up. Would Will still play guitar now, like this, before going the way of the dog and its doctor? It would be a shame if he didn't.

After scooping up the money, Sean went to his room and filled his backpack with what changes of clothes he'd held onto when he'd wound up in this fix, along with a couple paperbacks he'd grabbed at the nearby drop-in center. He left the shack, walked to the road, and caught the first ride out of town he could thumb down. As the countryside rolled by, he noticed a body lying out in a damp field. The crows were out, but they hadn't gathered around it, like they had the sense to stay clear. Sean didn't bother mentioning it to the driver.

Just Chew Your Way Out

One

Look, when I say *Let that bastard die*, I don't mean *Let the next sad asshole step into my old place and keep him alive*.

Revenge is just making up for a costly delayed reaction, except with better planning. I've had a long time to plan my revenge. Every man and woman in the supply caravan rumbling through that ravine down there is in my way, so they gotta die.

From my hiding place in the crags, I count five wagons, each with three armed guards, all probably crack-shots with those speed-reload crossbows strapped across their chests. The train's got two horsemen at either end, all stout, solid jackbooted Imperial leather-daddies, with broadswords bigger than they are hanging from their backs. Those guys don't worry me. That lean, hooded rider in the lead could be trouble, though, the one with a snaky, alert, no-bullshit posture atop that giant draft horse he rides. I'm not in the mood to see what engravings he's etched in the metal of his blade within the scabbard.

Still, he's all weighted down in Imperial regalia, and here's me, moving free and limber across the ridge, the way

I like, wearing only cargo-shorts and heavy-duty black leather boots. Maybe I overdid it with the night-vision eye-drops. I have to wear wyvern-rider goggles just so those wagon-torches don't scorch my eyes out of the sockets. There won't be much honest fighting tonight. No one's up here in the shadowed ridges but me...well, other than those scouts they sent to make sure the way was clear. But fuck those guys. They're dead. By now, I hear, so are most of the citizens left in New Spiralla. They've spent the last few weeks starving without medical supplies.

For a moment, I wonder what the place smells like by now. If I never smell New Spiralla again, I'll still probably never get that rancid zombie-piss stink out of my nose. This isn't about the smell, though. It's not about caring whether I'm the good guy or the bad guy here. This is about what Priest King Macose's betrayal cost me.

This last month ain't been hard, sleeping in the caves and cliff-side huts the locals used to inhabit...locals I was first hired to fight off. I was good at it, too. There was a time, the people of that city-state used to parade me around through their streets like I was some kind of hero. Even now, those memories are sorta nice. Such times now feel like a hazy past-life recollection.

Two

Like most people Spirelights move in with, those farmers and prospectors didn't much like it when their new neighbors started throwing their weight around. Can't blame 'em, but they're also the ones who kept trying to kill me while I was passing through. Mostly they were descended from bandits who hid in the ranges, mated with whatever women they could steal, and killed off the indigenous pygmies. I don't know who the pygmies killed off whenever they settled the region.

When old Priest King Macose wanted to hire my sword and magic tricks against the local trouble, I said "Sure, why not?" I didn't mention what I'd really come looking for. Rumors went it was hidden somewhere in the New Spiralla temple, at least according to some drunks in that tavern in Finiston. Spirelight fighters are nasty pieces of work, scarlet-blonde holy warriors to the core, with no sense of humor. I wouldn't want to piss one off. But the ones in New Spiralla were depleting like everything else there, so I came in handy. It might've been easier to make friends with the other side and just sack the damn place, but the Spirelights were the only folks for miles around with any good music. East Asterland really is that big a cultural sinkhole.

The temple looked and smelled more like a rundown drinkhall than a place for a Priest King to hold court. You know how these crumbling civilizations get during those last gasps of fading glory. What I'd come for was there, though, somewhere. I could feel it. It was just a matter of proving my mettle, then holding the gig, gaining the pompous old windbag's trust so he gave me the run of the place. Then it would be just a matter of time and sneaky searching.

After the first few skirmishes, Macose really took a liking to me. Funny to recall, I got pretty fond of the old bastard for a while. When you spend your days running an under-equipped guerrilla counter-insurgency through barren ranges full of enemies who were born with the salty mescal dust in their noses, it's nice to have such an appreciative boss who likes to stay up, get you drunk and shoot the shit with you.

All my old troubadour gigs had nothing on the rock star these folks made of me. I could probably even have had the run of the temple maidens and gotten away with it…if I hadn't had Rowan on the brain. I even wound up telling Macose all about her. Macose always looked like a giant peeled hardboiled egg to me, with barely useful marshmallow-slab limbs dangling like a rag doll's, slimy yellow hair puffing out of the top of his head like puss oozing over those watery eyes and frog mouth, propped on his throne like most such decadent monarchs, a pudgy, petulant overgrown child trying to play petty tyrant. As I talked, though, he swelled up so regally, I could almost see the majestic ruler of his glory days, before his alabaster warrior-king's build went to sod and New Spiralla faded into the dust of those foothills where it nestled.

It was his rightful pride, he said, at having a rare, extraordinary young man such as me in his service. "Like a knight in the great old tales," he sighed, "on a quest to reawaken his enchanted slumbering princess…the strong, feisty, highborn maiden, who falls in love with a handsome young rogue, no less. Yet here you've paused in this quest, to come to us in our hour of need."

Yeah, I know. The guy really talked like that. I swear, I couldn't make this shit up! Still, you should have heard the rhythm and cadence in his voice. I'll give the Spirelights this, they know how to bellow the lofty idealism so you want to believe it. I reminded Macose that I was just there 'til the situation was under control, which shouldn't take much longer.

"But beware the charms of sleeping princesses, Cassias my boy," he said. "You go on dreaming your waking dreams as you fly off on your wild quest. But remember, the princess dreams also, beneath the spell...and dreams deeper. Who knows what realms her dreams draw her to? When you draw her back from the void, you don't know what she'll bring back with her, or where that shall draw her anew through this waking life."

"Yeah, well..." I leaned back in that immaculate chair and took another snort of top-shelf royal whiskey. "I guess we'll just see."

Oh, I knew what he was really getting at. I was supposed to come to my senses, abandon my self-serving quest over a girl, realize my true calling, my true duty, stay here as the Champion Sword-Mage of New Spiralla. I just kept drinking and talking about Rowan. Priest King Macose just smiled and shook his head, in that bittersweet way old men sometimes do, when they hear young men going on like that, making silly, starry-eyed asses of ourselves.

"New Spiralla *can* rise again, over time," he said. "Our people won't fade into the night, Cassias. You won't let us."

He kept asking about the etchings in the palm of my right hand. That's when I should have known something was off. A bit about those etchings: they line up with those on my sword handle. When the two press together, it creates a synergy that magnifies every deadly muscle memory reflex in my body a thousandfold...and I've had a lot of those beaten into me. It also turns the blade into an extension of my arm, more or less literally. I carved both renditions of the pattern myself, my palm and the sword handle.

Here's what you might not get about Spirelights, though: they're *real big* on racial distinction between folks, particularly when it comes to magic. Yeah, I know, wherever you go, you have all these rules about who is and isn't allowed to learn what spells and traditions, based on your class, rank, race, affiliation, sexual orientation, all that horseshit. Whenever I decide to learn something new, I like telling the rule-keepers to shove it up their ass. I figured I could be honest with the Priest King, considering my unique mix of skills was keeping his little city-state from being overrun. To the Spirelight mind, though, there's no distinction between *socially acceptable* and *metaphysically possible*. I didn't realize the number it did on his mind, whenever I opened my mouth. Just by accomplishing everything I had, I'd become a being that couldn't possibly exist. Yet there I was.

Three

It's true, I really did fall in love with a feisty princess, *a woman above my station* and all that shit. We met at one of my stand-up gigs, in a tavern on the outskirts of the Frisha Kingdom. I might have actually stuttered when she caught my eye, halfway through the performance. I had everyone laughing, but her silver chuckle was the only one that stood out. I followed the sound straight to a voluptuous mouth that always looked thirsty for mischief, sharing a smooth heart-shaped face with the darkest, sharpest eyes

I'd ever seen. While everyone else slouched or leaned or stood around, she sat up straight at the bar, her arms crossed proudly beneath those glorious breasts of hers. Her strong, thick legs were crossed easily but not lazily. I don't think Rowan ever had a lazy bone in her body.

"Y'know," she said when we sat together afterwards, "it kinda sucks that you made me laugh so much. Now I feel obligated to call off those guards waiting to arrest you outside." She leaned closer. "That crack you made about running off to the hills with me thrown over your shoulder as a hostage." I stared, confused. The lower she whispered, the sultrier her voice got. "Talk of kidnapping royalty isn't taken lightly around here, especially not these days. So now I have to risk blowing my cover, *if* you want me to order 'em to leave you alone."

I looked her over, called to mind public pictures I'd seen. It should have been obvious. She wore those slum-girl rags and britches with way more thought-out, put-together style than any actual slum-girl. "Aw, shit," I said. "Wow, so..."

"Yeah." Her eyes widened and she nodded rapidly, so I'd make sure to keep it between us.

"Right," I said. "About those local guards – you mean the ones in the alley out back, rollin' around in the mud, trippin' their brains out with no idea why, thanks to how my vocal rhythms jacked with their brain frequencies?"

She only looked taken aback for a second. Then her eyes narrowed, she leaned her chin on her hand, and her smile widened. "Hmmmm, a man who thinks of everything. For future reference, though, our local police know some magic tricks of their own."

"Not like mine. Ain't legal for soldiers – or anyone –

to know the tricks I know."

"You're a long way from Imperial jurisdiction, you know."

"Yeah, that was the idea, headin' out this way. Some say that won't last, though."

"I'm hoping it will, but as things look lately...Well, you already know all that." She nodded at the stage where I'd just spent an hour spewing political bile. "Y'know, you're savvier on local issues than a lot of folks who grew up here."

"Hey, I just listen to the word on the road. Gotta keep the material current an' relevant, y'know."

"Well, you don't clean up half bad for a scraggly little barbarian mage-bard. If you actually plan to abduct me and ride off into the hills, you'd *better* charge a higher ransom than what you named on stage. Just so you know, though, members of the royal family are trained in hand-to-hand combat soon as we're old enough to walk. I'll buy you a drink while you think it over."

Four

It turned out, the Frisha royal family was so torn apart with back-stabbing in-fighting, that their daughter fucking a traveling troubadour who's also an outlaw sorcerer-swordsman-for-hire was the least of their worries. Her uncle, now feuding for the throne with her distant cousin since her parents' assassination, still wouldn't have liked it so much if she'd brought it up.

"So maybe that distant cousin would take a more

progressive outlook," I eventually asked her, "about us, I mean?"

"He just might...especially once we tell him about all those connections of yours, in the bandit hills. You could call in those guys, in his favor."

"Yeah, then there's my own sword and magic tricks."

She frowned and lowered her eyes.

"Wha – Aw, c'mon, you know I can handle myself."

"Yeah, just...Look, you've only seen a little of how ugly this feud can get."

"Hey, if I wasn't here, I'd probably be mixed up in something just as ugly somewhere else." I stroked her cheek. "And nowhere near as worth it. Besides, hey, I'm still savin' my real *sword with magic tricks* for you, honey."

"Pervert."

"Got a problem with that all of a sudden?"

"I'll let you know if I think of a reason to."

We talked it over more and agreed the smart idea was to back her cousin Snickersnack. *For us, our future together*...Not exactly a phrase I'd ever expected to enter my vocabulary. Once we started plotting with Snickersnack, and things actually started working out...Well, I might have been giddy, except she managed to keep me out of the direct fighting. I ain't the kind of bastard who feels good, sending other guys out to die without putting my own ass on the line. More importantly, me staying out of the fight didn't mean it wouldn't find its way to her.

I'd known about the etching ritual – what I've done to my hand and sword – for a while. It always sounded pretty badass. But you never realize the discipline, the concentration, the *motivation* needed to put yourself through something like that, 'til you have it. Normally, bluntly, I just ain't that kind of badass. Except all of a sudden I was, or felt like I could be. Because she brought it out in me, all the focus and motivation I needed and then some.

Think you might have what it takes? First, make sure you have the right pattern. Don't stop meditating over it 'til you're damn sure it's as deeply engraved in your brain as you mean to engrave it in your best weapon and yourself. Once you start cutting, don't look away 'til you're done. Don't even blink. If you slip up even a little, your arm will swell up and explode like a pork wiener held over a fire too long. Good thing I carved the sword handle first, 'cause I damn near bled to death when I worked on my palm.

I knew Rowan would object, so I made sure she didn't find out 'til afterwards. You should have heard her chewing me out when she saw my bandaged hand, the rest of my arm still caked in drying red. She wouldn't calm down when I explained how it benefited her. If anything, that pissed her off worse. I explained how it increased my own chances of survival. That worked a little better.

I wish I had a better story, about the first time I got to try out my new powers in a real fight, how I *felt the new power surge through me, more alive than ever in my howling new blood-lusting prowess and invulnerability.* I was out alone at night, cut through an alleyway, and a whole pack of assassins jumped me. Rowan's uncle sent them, we found out later. I'd have found out sooner, by keeping one of them alive and making him talk, but the sword wouldn't let me. Once it was out, it wouldn't be still 'til it drank its fill. Maybe that's when I should have realized the real reason Rowan freaked out so bad about what I'd done to myself for her.

I was already known for being someone you don't fuck with, so they sent a lot of them, more than I could have taken before. It felt…I can't say it felt *no* different than any other fight, but that's how it seems now. You ever get that, when you hit a super-accelerated height of mastery, like you've picked a lock in your brain, so it all falls into place? I can tell you about *after* the first time. The pounding in my skull died off steadily, and I noticed there were a lot of corpses bleeding all over the place, most of them missing bits and pieces, and I'd expended about a third of the usual energy, with hardly a scratch to show for it.

That other ceremony was her idea...the one where she needed to go under, go deep, leave that sweet body of hers for a while as not much more than a corpse. It was the only way to directly contact the particular pantheon of spirits we needed, one that just might turn the tide of the conflict. I still tried talking her out of it. You couldn't trust spirits who only let you make deals while out of body, with your soul itself at their mercy.

"Ah c'mon, Cass, you know me. I could talk my way out of the yellow plague." She actually had once, that's the funny thing. "This bunch is just shy, that's all. I'll have the whole pantheon eating out of my hand."

"While you don't have a hand to eat out of."

"Exactly."

So what could I do but trust her judgment? It wasn't the spirits she slipped up with, though. One of the temple maidens she brought into the ritual was a false friend with an old grudge. This turncoat knew how to land Rowan in an out-of-body coma, but she didn't know how to undo the spell. If she'd known, she'd have talked way before I finally let her die. No, really, she would have, trust me.

Five

It took me over a year, scouring land and sea, researching whatever, wherever I could, figuring out what had to be done to let Rowan reunite with her physical self and wake up. We needed a very specific combination of rare stones, arranged around the sleeper just so, while reciting the reclamation incantations, with the right vocal rhythm. Collecting all these stones took another half a year. I'd traced the last of them to Priest King Macose's kingdom, such as it was. Now all I had to do was kill Macose's enemies 'til I found the stone and smuggled it out of there. That, and I'd have a nice cash bonus to start Rowan and me afresh, most of the royal family's fortune having burned up in infighting expenses and all.

But Spirelights have a cute little myth about their kinds' origins. It goes something like this. Back in their home realm – called Deschemb, or something – their ancestors wandered into a seemingly deserted city and wound up as punk-bitches to the demons infesting the place. A few centuries later, some closet scholar kid made friends with the shining Gods of the Spirah Pantheon, who filled him with their happy fucking light that let him banish the demons from his people. They made of that ancient necropolis the Sacred City of Spiralla. Their new gods sent them out to make the world theirs. Folks didn't take kindly to divine subjugation, and man o'man, you've *never* heard a breed of martyrs who can whine about it like these guys! Someone finally chased 'em out of their own realm, across a vast black ocean, they say. Here in the temple of New Spiralla, there rose a big strutting statue of that scholar kid who'd first banished the demons. He held aloft a pair of twin curved short swords. Wouldn't you know, up there embedded in the pommels of those stone blades were these glistening honey-colored gems, just what I'd been looking for. Now I just needed a chance to climb up and pry one loose.

Thing is, though, I got along so well with old Macose, I figured, maybe I should just be honest, explain things over some drinks. He might say, *Why sure, ol' Cass, go right ahead. Take a stone. It's just a statue. You're talking about True Love.* Sure.

The conversation never got that far, though. I hadn't had so much as a full mug before I felt past my limit. Then I passed out. I woke up naked in the deepest, slimiest, smelliest dungeon they'd managed to dig in that dry, rocky gully. I'd never imagined rocks so utterly barren of mystical properties. Imagine trying to draw a lightning bolt through rubber walls. So no point trying to conjure anything to help me escape. Macose didn't visit me 'til I was too starved to stand, let alone strangle him. He was sorry to do this to me, he said. He really did have a lot of love for me. By now, I could barely lift my hand, but I managed a middle finger just for him. He kept stammering, something on the tip of his tongue like, *I love you like a son.* Of course he couldn't say that. I wasn't a Spirelight. It'd be like admitting he'd fucked a monkey.

Bottom line, I had a unique, seemingly impossible combination of abilities. He'd talked it over with his fellow clerics. They agreed my blood had a pretty good chance of resurrecting that punk kid messiah of theirs. They'd starved me physically and magically, to make absolutely sure I couldn't put up a fight. There's one ability they couldn't take away, though, and that's meditation. So while I was locked up, I meditated on the Spirelight language. None of the citizens of New Spiralla would speak in their sacred ancestral tongue in my presence, no matter how much they'd kissed my ass, buttering me up for the slaughter. Not even Macose would ever guess that I already knew it. But I did...backwards and forwards.

Finally, the day came. They dragged me up from my cell, splayed me out on a stone altar, and sacrificed me. First they rubbed me down with a gelatinous salve, some special Spirelight medicinal formula. It seeped deep into my pores, through my bloodstream, flooding me with a tingling sensation. Once it set in, someone cut a straight line down my center and spread me open from groin to sternum. Someone else reached in, carefully lifted out all my internal organs, and draped them over either side, across the exposed meat of my slit edges. I could lift my head and roll my eyes around, just enough to see them arranging the organs, in a pattern that matched the surrounding torches. When my gaze rolled back, I saw the towering edifice of that legendary Spirelight liberator-hero with his twin swords. I could only see one of those gems glittering in one of the sword-pommels.

So who should come striding up behind the altar, face so serene, but my old buddy Priest King Macose. He didn't mind speaking the sacred Spirelight language in my presence now. They had no plans to let my body die. I felt it gathering around me, the spirit they'd summoned so it could possess my meat-sack. They'd removed my organs, but hadn't detached them. The spirit had to enter through my exposed guts. Macose lifted a ritual blade over me, to puncture each organ one at a time, so this spirit's tendrils could leak in. My blurring eyes recognized the blade...my blade. It was my turn to gape at a metaphysical impossibility. That sword hates everyone except me. Any other dude who draws it is likely to slip and cut his own dick off. I still don't know how Macose fought it into submission. He leveled it over me, tip downward. I listened to the incantations he spoke, all about saving his people from the decadence to which this world had pulled them, so they might rise up to new vitality, guided by the being soon to inhabit the sacred vessel that was me.

Our people won't fade into the night, Cassias. You won't let us.

All around, his white-hooded acolytes chanted after him, in a droning call-and-response. I drew the deepest breath I could manage, and let it out in the same words Macose had said. Except backwards. As in from b-a-c-k-w-a-r-d-s to s-d-r-a-w-k-c-a-b. In Spirelight, it translated to *No. They can't have me. I'm free of them.* Let *them all die. Starting with him.*

As soon as the words passed my lips, Priest King Macose froze up. His face drew long. My sword slipped from his fingers and clattered at his feet, then he let out a great, rolling, belching god-fart and filled his robes with his own guts. Torches flared and spewed molten showers, pelting the acolytes as they shrieked and ran everywhere in a panic, trampling each other. All that metaphysical juice I'd been denied surged through me. Normally, it would make me the peppiest bastard you ever saw, dancing all over the place. Right now, I was still weak from starvation and dehydration, I'd lost a lot of blood, and my guts were still all over the place. I had to scoop them back in as best I could, situate them properly as I knew how, and pull myself shut. Eventually I sat up, not daring to let go of my sliced abdomen.

Ironically, I later realized, it was that magic Spirelight salve that saved my life. I don't care what you've heard, *no one's* badass enough to scoop their own guts back in, hold themselves shut, slide off a blood-slick altar, find their sword, get it back in the scabbard, and crawl away into the darkness amidst all the pandemonium, not without some magical help. I crawled into some hovel somewhere, curled up and hid there shivering for a while. When my arms gave out and fell away from my abdominal cavity, it stayed shut. The magic salve held me together like glue.

I won't say I wished I was dead, but I wasn't loving life much either. I hadn't brought that last stone home to Rowan, though, so I held on. First, I had to get out of the ranges surrounding New Spiralla. Once I wasn't such a mess, I'd come back for what I needed, and I wouldn't play nice this time.

Six

As for all those stones, I hadn't bet everything on myself. Whenever I found one, I'd either brought it home personally or sent it to Rowan's cousin by a trusted messenger. I was on Resurrect Rowan detail, but he knew how to perform the ritual and what missing pieces to look for if I died trying. It wasn't 'til the ship voyage that I actually thought *I'm gonna die.*

I stowed away, stayed below deck the whole time, too weak to lift my sword, and the fever set in. My gut wound puffed up like a fat shiny worm under a thin layer in the center of my torso. Damn, did it itch! I poked some holes in it and squeezed out clear jelly pus 'til it flattened out. I swear, I must have squeezed a quarter of my body weight in pus onto the floor. Once it quit oozing, it started gnawing at the edges, burning in the middle. The sea was stormy for half the voyage. I got tossed around so much, between the crates where I hid, I thought I'd split back open. I finally managed to crawl inside a crate, bound for my destination, to smuggle myself off the ship.

Three weeks later, I reached the edge of the kingdom. My vision was full of fog. It was all I could do to get to the saloon and toss the latest coins I'd managed to steal at an innkeeper. I dragged my ass upstairs, found the room number matching the key he gave me, and passed out. The next afternoon, I was downstairs in the saloon, trying to choke down some breakfast and keep it from coming back up, when an old buddy of mine came in and recognized me. The best luck I'd counted on was *no one* recognizing me. The Spirelights had shaved me bald as a baby for the sacrifice, my hair was just now sprouting again, and I was still skin and bones.

But sure enough, here came ol' Crackerface over from the bar. Everyone calls him that, which is even funnier since he's black. He looked back and forth from me to the drink in his hand, like, *I ain't that drunk yet. Someone spike this when I wasn't looking, so now I'm seein' shit?* Finally he said, "Cass…?"

I managed to nod.

"Well fuck me gently with a prunin' blade, if it ain't –"

"Keep your voice down," I rasped.

"Aw," he huffed, "you ain't gotta worry 'bout that. Feud's over." He sat across from me. "Damn, man, what happened to you?"

"You don't wanna know. How'd the feud wrap up?"

"Duke Snickersnack's finally on his way to a coronation. After that last alliance he struck, Lord and Lady Frisha decided to cave."

"'Bout fuckin' time. Still got that wagon of yours?"

"Sure."

"Could you maybe throw me in the back and get me to the South Frisha Chateau? I got some important news, about breaking the spell on Rowan..."

"Oh. Shit. Man." His face sank. "Look, Cass, word was, you got your ass killed, somewhere in the East Asterland ranges. Something about the feuds around New Spiralla."

"Yeah, sure, whatever. I'll explain later. Rowan still safe? That fuckwit cousin of hers bothered keepin' the crypt guarded while he was busy becoming king?"

"Cass. Rowan's been awake for like six months. Turns out, whatever spirits she went out of body to get hold of, well, they liked her a lot and agreed to help. They showed up before she did, back to this realm I mean. That's what turned the tide."

"Yeah...aw hell yeah, of course she pulled it off! That's my girl. Can't keep her down." I shook with joy, thinking of my darling back among the living, back in this crazy war called life.

"She still had to...Look, man, I don't get how all that

political shit works. Somethin' to do with gettin' the backing Snickersnack needed from the Empire. They've had their eye on the nation for a while, you know, waffling on throwing him their support. Some Imperial affiliate got sweet on her at some diplomatic party, and…well, they got married last week. It was a big thing. They threw a carnival and everything. Such a ragin' party, it didn't die off 'til a day or so ago. Half the city's still sleepin' it off."

For the first time, I noticed something. This was the same saloon where I'd met Rowan. The place hadn't changed much. Once Crackerface's words sank in, I just wanted to crawl back to my room and finish dying. If I was lucky, my spirit would hover around, watch the innkeeper and everyone start wondering what had happened to that sadsack in the room near the end of the hall. First they'd get twitchy when I wouldn't answer the door. Then the smell would start leaking out. They'd break the door down and get hit in the face with the voided bowel fumes. They'd blink their watering eyes clear and see my bloated corpse giving everyone the finger. But I'm too much of a stubborn fuck to just putter out like that. I had to know Rowan was really okay, that this hoity-toity political marriage wasn't something she'd been steamrolled into.

She'd never been one to let herself get shoved around like that, but politics are a weird, slimy thing. While we're at it, I was curious how the hell her cousin had managed to resurrect her without me.

Once I got some strength up, I visited the South Frisha Chateau. The first thing I saw was the happy couple, strolling hand in hand through the sunlit gardens. I started towards them, with no idea what I'd say or do. Then she leaned her head on his shoulder, in a way you just can't fake. The sight felt like an energy wave hitting me in the chest and pushing me back into the shadows. Now I know how demons feel when some asshole hangs a protective charm over the front door.

So that was it for me and the Frisha kingdom. She was happy. Good for her. Sooner or later, I'd get around to letting her know I was still kicking. If I couldn't have her back, I was damn well gonna have my old self back. Except I never could, not completely. To remember that, all I had to do was look at my palm, at the labyrinthine pattern carved into my flesh. I glanced down at the magic sword on my belt, with the matching pattern carved in the handle. Oh well, it would come in handy. After all, there was still a world full of trouble to get into.

Seven

What I needed was someplace to get myself back in fighting shape. It turns out, good ol' Crackerface had me covered, him and all our crazy old militia pals. With me as a middle-man, they'd whored out their fighting arms to Duke Snickersnack's bid for the crown. Now they were back to hiding and training in their ragtag camp off in the woods, the new regime's dirty little secret, sharpening their swords and arrowheads for whenever the next uprising happened. They were glad to take me in. Soon as I was back in shape, and the local sawbones said the last of the infection was out of my system, I heard the open road calling my name. Before long, I picked up on the latest gossip about New Spiralla.

STORY TIME WITH CRAZY UNCLE MATT

Apparently, Priest King Macose can't leave his throne room, has all sorts of vines growing up his ass and all through him, their juices keeping him alive. Such vines will have bonded with his skeleton. If he doesn't have leaves sprouting from under his fingernails, he will soon enough. His kingdom hasn't fared much better.

No one can spin a sob story like a leader of Spirelights, like how mean ol' me magically prolapsed his ass *for no reason*, just like the locals here were giving him trouble, like the original natives who burned Old Spiralla to the ground and drove his people out of Deschemb. So the Empire's been lending its support, ferreting in food, fresh clothes, education, military training, you name it. Seemed Macose swung some favors for someone in high places, and he's been calling it in, for his people's time of need. That's not okay with me, and I know this territory like few outsiders.

The first caravan I took out, I let 'em get as far as the dugout offshoot from the river, feeding the town's irrigation. I piled the corpses into that waterway, then I went scouting out other such branch-offs. Since getting back to the Asterland ranges, that's as close as I've gotten to New Spiralla. Along with leaving the drinking water not so fresh, it's fucked whatever crops still grew within a mile of the city walls. All the good game's fled upriver. For the last month, whenever I catch another caravan coming through, I make sure it doesn't reach its destination. Scavenging the remains keeps me stocked in food and water. Here comes this latest one, rolling along, right on schedule.

Next to my foot, there's a spike driven into the ground with a taut cord tied to it. I yank that spike loose. The cord whip-snaps then zips away like a snake, scraping sparks from a line of flint edges. Both sides of the ravine light up with a chorus line of explosions. Great balls of fire spill downhill like flaming boulders that smack the wagons. The crash rolls uphill, shaking loose more charred dirt and rock. The impact shivers up my legs. Half the guys in there never know what hits 'em. The others run around on fire, shrieking like flailing banshees. Some of them scramble up the hillside. My sword sings free and slices them right out of their misery. One of them spills back downhill like an extra fireball. The others drop and finish cooking at my feet.

This ravine must look like a giant roaring fire pit for miles around. The ranges blaze with shrieking life and death at their most gloriously merciless. I almost wish I hadn't pulled this off so well, so my sword arm could get in a *real* workout. My blade's never been thirstier, nor my senses sharper.

Only one of them escapes unscathed. He almost manages to sneak up on me. I spin and spot him mounting the ridge, a few yards off...the leader who caught my eye as someone who might live to give me a real fight. His blade's already out. Hey, what do you know, so is mine! I spring and close half the distance. He stays put. At first, I figure he's spooked by how raving nuts I must look, or he's just playing it cool-headed and cautious.

"Cass?"

Now it's my turn to pause. That's not a dude's voice. I lower my blade a little, but not much, 'cause I don't quite believe my ears. She pushes her hood back. I pull up my goggles to be sure. The firelight hurts my eyes. The night-vision eye-drops have worn down enough, though, so I don't go blind. She probably can't decide what to process first: that I'm still alive, or that I'm the lone bandit who's been starving out New Spiralla.

Finally she says, "What the fuck are you doing?"

"Nice to see you too, baby. What the fuck are *you* doin'?"

"Trying to help a friend who saved my life...and maybe, just maybe find out personally who doesn't want my friend helped."

"Huh – Wha – Wait, hold up, you mean that fucking Priest King?"

"Yes!" She never was one to sit on the sidelines like a good little high-born maiden, trained to fight since she could walk and all. That's my girl. Except she's not anymore.

"*Saved your life?*"

"Yeah, while you ran off to do your thing, wherever or whatever that was, as usual."

"I'm the one who's lucky to be alive after what that motherfucker put me through." My finger stabs the hot, smoky air between us and New Spiralla. "*I was the one running all over the damn place lookin' for the pieces that'd bust you out of that spell that turncoat skank of a temple maiden put on you.* I was gonna steal the final piece I needed from Macose, but he had me turned inside out like a fuckin' trout first." *After I told him all about the fix she was in, the mission I was on.* Then there was that missing gem in the statue while I was on the altar. "By the time I got back, you were already up and had yourself a cute little perfumed prince of a husband. Figured it was time for me to hit the road."

"You're the one who gutted Macose," she says.

"I – What – *Well, yeah!* What, did you just *not hear* everything else I just said?"

"Cass, I…Look, I didn't know!"

"Okay, so now you do. So you gonna help me finish wipin' out those corrupt, degenerate shitfucks or what?"

"*No!*"

"Huh?"

"I said no. Look, Cass, Priest King Macose sent his personal envoy to see my cousin, with the final stone in the assembly needed to let my spirit back into my body, and –"

"Yeah? So how you think he found out about that?"

Her face tightens. "It doesn't matter now. It can't. It's too big. I married into the Empire because my cousin's new kingdom needs the Imperial support. So does New Spiralla. We struck the deal with the Empire to nurse the Spirelight nation back to health. And here you are, out to fuck the whole thing up."

"*Out to?* Baby, *I'm just gettin' warmed up!*"

"Walk away."

"Oh, I'll *walk away*, all the way to New Spiralla. Then I'm gonna finish what I started, with all my guts where they belong inside me this time."

"Those were good people down there you just killed, good soldiers. I should still kill you right here. I'm telling you now, just once, *just turn around and go.* I'll take care of all the bounties on your head. Just go."

By now, I'm shaking and boiling so bad, I can barely move. In the grip of a tremoring, teeth-chattering rage like this, there's only one way *to* move.

There's this torture-trick I've seen used. You put a rat in a wooden box with one end open, strapped to some poor bastard's stomach. You light the other end of the box on fire. As things heat up, all Mister Rat can do is to chew his way through. Right now, I know how that rat feels. The hottest blaze I feel ain't the flames from the ravine. It's everything I feel *behind me*, everything I've put myself through, over three damn years.

When I blink, I see Rowan's eyes bright with laughter, remember when nothing could be more important than making her smile, no sight sweeter than joy on her face. I'm right back there, in every happy memory we ever shared. Then I open my eyes, and there she is now. Maybe she's the one I should chew through. Or she'll chew through me. Let's find out.

I fly at her. She just stands there. I try to check myself. The etching in my palm is fused with that of the sword-handle, though. It doesn't let me stop. My sword point crunches through the weak spot in her armor, still so sharp I don't even feel it slide through her flesh and guts. There's a split second to hope like hell it hasn't, that maybe her armor stopped it after all. Then the sword's tip punches the back plate. She just falls against me, hiccups, and looks at me. I gape back at her. She shakes and gurgles. Her eyes roll back in her head, and she slides away, off my blade. I'm still shaking when she stops.

For a long time, all I can think is, *Did she* choose *not to fight back, or did she really just not think I had the balls?* Neither answer makes much sense. We knew each other too well. It's this blade and sword hand she didn't understand. Except, I remember, she did. I was the one who didn't. Either way, that's no spell she's lying there under this time.

The nearby raging blaze burns the shock out of my system. No room yet to mull over practicalities, like how big the bounty on my head's gonna be after this, let alone the grief and self-loathing. I start towards New Spiralla, brandishing the perfect sword for the job.

Useful Instincts

I wake up on the couch. It's cold in here, but I don't tug the blanket closer. I need to get sharp. The cold air helps with that. There's no real reason I have to be sharp. It's another few hours 'til I have to be at work. It's just an old instinct that comes and goes. It wakes up in me, wants to be useful again, not let anything convince me it's not 'til it goes back to sleep.

This is my living room. The bedroom with its big warm bed is just a door away. I had one of those nights where everything in me rebelled against the bed, the thought of it, like it would eat me if I lay down on it. Some nights I can't even sleep on the couch. Instead, I lie flat on the floor, hands folded over my chest like a vampire in a coffin. Sometimes I use the half-empty beanbag chair as a pillow. Other times, I let the back of my skull lie like a rock that's rolled to a stop. In times like that, this whole apartment feels unnatural around me, this wide, clean space for which I pay five hundred a month without much trouble.

Why complain? Plenty of folks would gladly trade. I used to be one of those people. Well shit, if that's how I really feel, maybe I should go make one of them an offer. My younger self mutters at me, *Wow, buddy, I wish I had your problems*. Maybe I'm addicted to this quieter life. So here I am, trapped in one addiction, writing in withdrawal from another. Whatever wandering bum I traded with would have to take my steady job, too, or one like it.

Through the half-open patio blinds, the world is white with snow, except for the shaded beams of the railing and the innermost shrubs. I remind myself how much it sucked, having to sleep outside during such weather.

I stand up and stretch myself into proper erect posture, which I don't do much anymore. It feels weird, like I've become impossibly tall. The cluttered coffee table and the couch seem miles beneath me, like I'm dangling from a towering cliff. I still have on my jeans and wife-beater from last night. My muscles feel thicker and tighter against the inner fabric than they did when I fell asleep. It must be the cold. I look again at the snow outside. I'll have to leave early to get to work on time through that mess. Good thing I'm getting myself together early.

I walk outside all bundled up, keeping my posture good. There's a girl bundled up thicker than I am. She carries out a bundle of some things, puts it in the back seat of her car, then she scrapes snow and ice off her windows. At first I can't tell a thing about her, except that she has very thin legs wrapped in faded jeans that are soaked at the ankles. She probably wears long johns under the jeans, and her legs probably look even thinner without them. Her bulky coat above those petite legs creates an incongruous effect, like a shaggy tree with a spindly trunk that's about to break in the wind. I can't see her face thanks to the giant, low-hanging hood. Then I spot a pair of bright eyes with giant batting lashes, surrounded by the smooth skin of a pretty young face, the mouth wrapped in a blue scarf. I walk slower as she climbs into her car and guns it to life.

The rear tires spray snow, but the car stays put. I walk to the front, dig my heels into the snow, grip the rim of the hood, and put all my sinews into the shove. It feels futile at first, then the car slides away from me. I draw up sharply and plant my feet, so I don't fall on my face. The car swings around and settles on snow that's been packed down tight by all the other cars that have made it out of this parking lot in the last few hours.

She rolls down her window and she peers out at me. "Thanks a lot," she says with a big, bright, embarrassed smile that's so shaky, it's almost a nervous laugh. "Are you okay?"

"Yeah, no problem." She's trying to get a sense of me, so I do my best to make my eyes and smile as bright and winning as hers. "I just hope I can get to work on time."

"Are you walking?" she asks incredulously.

"Yeah." My smile widens with good-humored embarrassment.

I must be pathetic enough, or dashing enough, or somehow both, something she decides is non-threatening, because she says, "You need a ride somewhere?"

It's either this or a half-mile slog, praying I catch the bus on time. Must be my lucky day. I tell her where I work and ask if she's going that way. She says she'll drop me off, and I climb into the front passenger seat next to her. Her hood's pushed back now, and she's still as pretty as I first thought. Her face is long with a pointed nose. Her coat's open and pushed back because she has the heat on in the car. When she leans forward, I see that her back is very toned, very smooth and flat beneath her neck. For some reason, this feature makes me drool the most. I glance in the back seat at the bundle she brought out. A stack of formal documents has slid partly into view. I think they might be medical documents for some reason. They look crumpled and old. I make some small talk, but she keeps looking at me funny.

"You're familiar from somewhere," she says.

"You've probably seen me around the building," I say.

"I don't live in the building. My boyfriend does."

"Oh. So how come he wasn't out helping you get your car loose?"

"He has a leg injury. He has to walk with a cane. This weather's been hell for him. He goes outside as little as possible."

"That sucks. I hear it's supposed to clear up by the end of the weekend."

"I hope so."

She drops me off at work and drives away. As soon as she's gone, I remember where we've seen each other before, or at least I think so. I laugh nervously, a little maliciously. No wonder I didn't recognize her, bundled up like that.

It was back in August. The girl I'm thinking of had on a white tank-top that was too small even for her and a pair of green shorts that barely covered her ass. She kept her hair pulled back in a ponytail. I was walking home from the bus stop, past the tennis courts between the bus and the apartment, and the heat was doing nothing for my already foul mood. The tennis courts in the summer are full of hot girls like that, which always made for at least something pleasant about the trudge home. I miss it in fall and winter.

I spied her through the fence, darting nimbly back and forth, swinging a racket, wearing what might have been a cheerful grin or a grimace of exertion. At the other side of the court was one of those preppy, slick-blonde assholes in a T-shirt with elbow-length sleeves, made of thick white material that looked hot as a parka in that weather. You could tell it was expensive material just by looking at it, which I guess is what matters to that kind of douchebag. I stopped thinking about either of them, because I realized I needed to piss. I crossed the grassy mound between the tennis courts, past a picnic table, towards the stone structure with the public bathrooms for the players.

Somehow Preppy-Boy fouled a shot horridly, and the tennis ball flew wild. It soared all the way over the netting and bounced off my head. My skull rang a little, then I saw the ball bounce in the grass close to my feet. I growled, snatched it up, and chucked it hard back at Preppy-Boy. I missed him so the ball bounced off the fence next to his head. Maybe I shouted something like *watch it, asshole.* He shouted something back like *What the fuck's your problem?*

I realized it had been an accident, that he'd have probably shouted apologies instead of returned hostility if I hadn't been so hotheaded. I called out listlessly, "Sorry. I've just had a really shitty day."

Apparently he felt hotheaded, too, because he was already storming towards me. His girl ran up behind him to try to hold him back. It didn't work. "Yeah well, your day's about to get a lot shittier," he said. His tan, toned arms were tense. One of them cocked back to swing. It was an embarrassingly calibrated move.

I forgot my charitable notions and said, "No, yours is."

As he closed in, before he could swing, I sent a sharp kick straight into his kneecap. Bone and cartilage gave out under my heel with a ripping pop. His leg bent back unnaturally. His girlfriend started screaming. The sound disagreed with my head almost worse than the tennis ball had. Other people were looking around in confusion. It had all happened too fast for them to know what was going on.

I got the hell out of there pretty quickly after that. Whatever. I could find somewhere else to take a piss. No one came after me. I guess they were too busy with the guy whose leg I'd just busted. For the rest of my walk home, I kept expecting a police car or two to pull over next to me. For the next few weeks, I took a different route to and from work. Eventually, I got comfortable and complacent enough so I fell back into taking the old quicker way. I never encountered anyone who recognized me from that incident.

But it doesn't make sense for it to be the same girl. Her injured boyfriend lives in my building, she said. I haven't seen anyone in the building walking with a cane, or crutches beforehand for that matter. Someone like that would be hard to miss, especially since he'd surely recognize me. I get a funny mental picture of him coming at me again, this time swinging with his cane like a pissed off geriatric chasing kids off his lawn. Today it's a busy day on the line, though, so I forget about it by the time I clock out. A coworker gives me a lift home, and I'm glad to find the parking lot shoveled. I see the girl's car parked where it was this morning. At least I think it's the same car. I watch for her as I head to my door, but she's nowhere around. Once I'm locked inside, I sit on my couch and almost want to lie down, but I'm too restless. It's the old instinct, *insisting* I be restless. For once in too long, I have a reason to be. Or at least I think I might.

Someone knocks on my door. I jump a little, then I go

and look through the peephole. It's her. Now that I've spent some time replaying the tennis court incident in my mind, I open the door and I'm sure it's the same girl. I could have painted her face on the memory, but I somehow don't think so. When I look deep into her eyes, I can tell that she knows, how I'm the guy who crippled her boyfriend because I was having a bad day.

"Hi. Can I come in?" She says it like someone's been chasing her, but I know it's just the cold of the hallway she wants to get away from. I've turned the heat on in my place, but it isn't much warmer yet.

"Sure," I say and step aside.

She walks past me and lets her coat slide off her shoulders. She hangs it on the bar stool I keep next to the counter between my living room and the kitchenette. The shirt beneath has no neck, hangs loose, and I see that smooth, flat back like the spine stops beneath her neck and starts again somewhere inside the shirt.

"So what's up?" I say. "Can I get you a beer or something?"

"Do you have coffee?"

"Sure. I'll brew some. Have a seat on the couch."

I set some coffee brewing. She sits with her knees pressed tight, her head hunched, hands rubbing together, eyes darting left and right like she hopes to find a comforting idea about me from the sparse furnishings.

I walk over and sit on the other side of the couch. "So how'd you know which door was mine?"

"I saw you go in."

"Oh." I wonder where she was watching from, but I don't ask. Instead, I watch the shirt with no neck draped over her bony shoulders above that toned back. I'm polite on my side of the couch, when what I really want to do is pin her flat on the floor. Maybe I have the wrong idea, and this is a booty-call, and I'm being rude by *not* attacking her. Jesus, I'm out of practice! "So what do you want?"

"I'm not sure how to say it. This is weird."

"So just spit it out."

"It's not that simple."

"It never feels like it is, does it?"

She laughs in spite of herself. "No, I guess not. It's about my boyfriend."

"Oh. So I guess you told him *you found the bad man.* What, does he wanna press charges?"

"No. This is the part where it's hard to start. You used to work in a soap factory in Virginia, didn't you?"

It takes me a second, but then I remember. "Yeah. Well, I wasn't a steady worker. I was a transient then, and I signed up with a labor service that sent me there for a week."

"Yeah. So was Jeff, my boyfriend. He signed up with the same people and they sent him to the same factory."

I almost say *That preppy snot used to have to work factory jobs?* Instead, I just say, "I don't remember him."

"You wouldn't. He's a completely different person now. He was a junkie back then. He's cleaned up now, though, has a nice office job and everything. You should have seen him when we met. He was still pulling himself together. Sometimes he tells me he's gone soft, but I tell him he's being too hard on himself."

I remember that sloppy punch he started to throw, how he didn't see my move coming, how he squealed like a little bitch when I dropped him. I say, "So how's he holding up now?"

"He missed a lot of work. It was a good thing he had so much sick time saved up. He's missing more work, now that it's cold. But it's not really his injury keeping him in. Something else broke in him that day, besides his kneecap." She stares at me with something stranger than anger. "He remembers your face, from back then. He didn't realize it 'til he was down and staring up at you from the ground."

"He remembers me from the soap factory?"

Her eyes drop, then return to me. "No. That was my hunch. I didn't think you'd have been one of the laborers, though. I thought you'd have been a foreman or something."

"Why would you think that?"

She takes a deep breath. "Did you ever hear what happened to that place?"

"I heard something about them being shut down. I'd moved on by then, and barely recognized the name of the place when I read it in some online article. Something about the ingredients in their soap being fucked up, causing bad reactions in people who handled it."

"Did you ever use any of the soap from the place?"

"Yeah. At the end of one day, they handed out plastic bags full of samples. I used it in the shower that night at the cheap motel I was staying in. It made my skin itch like crazy, so I threw it away. I thought that was just me, though, at the time."

"You were lucky. I don't know what chemicals they were putting in that shit, but a lot of people had it a lot worse than you."

"People like your boyfriend, you mean. So what happened to him?"

"Something in the soap soaked into his skin, and it went to his brain. It started when he was asleep. At first, he thought it was just nightmares. Then he woke up, and the nightmares were still there."

"Sounds like a great acid-trip to me."

"Yeah, that's what he thought at first. He figured one of his junkie buddies had dosed him with something. Then he kept using the soap, and it kept happening. It was the doctors in the ER who finally helped him figure it out." Some weird kind of pride floods her voice. "My boyfriend was one of the people in the class action lawsuit that finally shut that place down. That's how he got the money to start over."

Even though the soap didn't effect me like that, I wish I'd kept up on all this at the time. I could have gotten in on the action, pulled some of that money. "Good for him," I say.

"Not really. Those chemicals are long gone from his system, but they permanently affected his brain chemistry. He still has nightmares from the hallucinations. He says demons are tearing him apart, and the demons have human faces. Some of them are old junkie friends from back in the day. Most of those guys are dead now. I couldn't help being glad about it, even though that's horrible of me."

"No, that's totally natural, at least in my opinion."

"Thanks," she says. "Maybe. But the rest of the faces he sees in his dreams are people from that factory. He wasn't sure, but I listened to him and suggested that, and he realized, yeah, some of them were. Now I wish I'd kept my mouth shut. Now he's obsessed with finding out what happened to everyone who had a hand in running the place, who poisoned him and the rest of the workers, like it's some demon conspiracy puzzle he can piece together, like he'll find Satan himself at the center of it. Lately, he's been having me use my job connections to track down all sorts of records about the factory, about the case."

Oh, I think. That must have been those files I saw in the back of her car. "And I'm one of the demon faces he always sees in his nightmares, even though he has no idea where he first saw me. Then the mean old *face out of the past* pops out of nowhere one day, his ego writes a check he can't cash, he gets his ass kicked, and now he's convinced that it's not all hallucinations, and I'm a demon in the flesh come to chase him around." I recite all that in a sing-song way.

She looks annoyed, then turns away embarrassed. "That's pretty much it." Then quickly, "He always had a loopy streak like that, but he kept it in line, never let it effect how he saw reality. It's just since...well..."

"Since that little fight with me, you mean."

"Yeah. Since then, he's gotten more and more isolated, and that loopy side gets more and more prominent, and he *is* letting it shake his hold on reality."

It sounds to me like he's long since shaken that off like fleas from a dog. "How many people has he been going around blabbing this shit to?"

"Just some of our friends. He kept it together well enough when he was still at work, but even they started hearing him say strange things."

"So why are you here telling me this?"

"I thought you had a right to know. He's getting weirder and weirder, and I don't know what he'll try when he feels more mobile."

Considering how it went when we all met, this doesn't

worry me too much. Still I ask, "You didn't tell him about running into me, did you?"

She sighs. "I did. I'm sorry. I wish I hadn't. I don't know why I did. I knew it was a bad idea even before I said it. Then he got *really* weird with me, and I had to get out of there. He's still up there, huddled in his apartment, still jabbering about you at the walls for all I know. I haven't been back there in hours."

"But you came back and waited for me to get home."

"Yeah."

"Look, if you're really scared, maybe you shouldn't be here at all. It sounds like he's a pretty sketchy guy to deal with."

"Yeah, but I really thought he'd gotten better, that he'd keep a grip. Then what happened, happened." She pauses. "You don't seem like you're all that stable yourself."

"Me, I'm harmless."

"I *know* that's bullshit."

"Look, about that day," I say. "He started it."

"Yeah, I know. I'm sorry."

"It's okay." I put a gentle hand on her shoulder. It startles her, but she doesn't pull away. "Sounds like you've been having a rough time lately. You deserve to have someone give you a break."

"Thanks. You've been really patient. I know how weird all this must seem."

I nod. "Like I said, it's okay. I've seen weirder."

"Back when you were a transient, like Jeff?"

"Yeah."

"Look, you know he probably only set eyes on you once or twice, and your face stayed in the back of his subconscious 'til the soap chemicals gave it something to do. I don't think any of this is your fault. Just so you know that."

"Thanks. My name's Sean, by the way. Sean Harris."

She laughs a little. "My name's Natalie. Good to meet you, Sean."

"Good to meet you too, I guess. I think that coffee should be ready by now. Still want any?"

She nods enthusiastically, so I get up and pour two cups. She wraps her hands around the steaming mug like she still needs to thaw out, even though the heater's long since warmed the place up by now. Finally she drinks her coffee. We make more small talk to defuse the rest of the tension. When I touch her shoulder again, she leans in and kisses me. I start to slide my arms around her, and she pulls back.

"I'm sorry," she says sharply. "I really didn't come over to – Look, it's just –"

"I know. It's fine."

I lean in and kiss her again. At first, her lips are still against mine, then hesitantly, she starts kissing me back. I kiss her deeper, harder. I pull her close for more. She responds nicely 'til my hands snake up under her shirt and find her small, plump breasts. She's not wearing a bra. When my fingers play with her nipples, she stiffens.

"What's wrong?" I ask.

She puts a gentle but firm hand on my chest. "I'm sorry. This is just too weird."

"I know. I shouldn't have –"

"No, it's not that, it's just..." She looks around at the living room. "Can we get out of here? I don't like this building right now. It's too full of his craziness, all the crazy shit he's been babbling about. He won't shut up. I'm sick of it. I know that sounds awful, with everything he's been through, but...Can we leave? Like...maybe go back to my place?"

My ethical side taps the brakes, thinking of poor old crazy Jeff upstairs, Jeff who used to work in the same crooked soap factory as me when we were both down and out, even though we never knew each other. It's not his fault he got the worst of the poison soap and it fucked him up so badly that he had to turn all the way into a yuppie with a chipped shoulder just to climb out of hell. It's not his fault he's still so crazy deep inside that his girlfriend's looking for comfort on the end of the dick of the man who crippled him, a man he thinks is a demon out to get him.

I guess I wouldn't want Natalie as a girlfriend, but hell, she smells great, she tastes great, she feels great, and it ain't like I'm planning to marry her. I follow that smooth toned back of hers towards the door 'til she slides the giant coat on over it, then I follow the giant coat. We get in her car, she starts driving, and the nice neighborhood falls away. She drives us out through snowed over cornfields, along roads that haven't been plowed so well. We have to go slower over all the ice and slush.

The further we go, the less anything feels like civilization or respectability. It feels more like the days when I drank a bottle of cheap scotch behind a gas station with a fellow day-laborer claiming he used to be a tattoo artist, trying to convince me I should get a tattoo of a demon fucking a nun up the ass. He spilled his guts about how his wife had kicked him out and he was gonna go shoot her and her lover. We finished the scotch, I made the wrong comment about his cheating wife, so he attacked me, and I wouldn't have been able to beat that man twice my size unconscious if it hadn't been for all that pure, savage, wonderful *adrenaline* burning the liquor in my veins. I don't know if that guy ever woke up, because that's when I skipped town and ended up working in a soap factory in Virginia.

I look Natalie over as she drives. Damn, she's hot. The waiting is killing me. I'm on fire with more than lust, with things that make the lust burn hotter. I'm not just off to get laid. I'm sneaking around with a haunted woman hiding from a delusional boyfriend, and I'm about to give him one more reason to want to kill me. Now I know why I woke up feeling like I needed to be sharp. All this, it's almost *better* than sex.

We pull into the shoveled driveway of a little house I guess is hers. She opens the front door and lets me walk in first. Seated on the couch is the man whose kneecap I busted months ago. He's really gone to shit, pale and jittery and thinner with bugged-out eyes like he was in the factory. I think, *Oh right. That guy.*

I look back at Natalie as she closes the door behind us. She smiles at me, then at her boyfriend. "I brought him for you, honey. He was even easier than I told you he'd be."

Jeff gets up, one hand leaning on his cane, the other pointing a .38 revolver at me. I know better than to stare and get hypnotized by the little black hole at the end of the barrel, like most people would. I look right into his bug eyes, and I know he'll shoot. His finger tightens on the trigger. The revolver's hammer leans back. I rush him, swatting his cane with one arm, my other arm knocking his gun as far from my face as possible. The shot snaps somewhere behind my head, and the gun falls out of his hand. I don't think it sounded that loud 'til I feel my ears ringing, a lot worse than they did when his tennis ball hit me. Jeff and Natalie both scream. Jeff falls on his ass. He stares past my legs. I turn around. Natalie stands there looking at us, her eyes dull with shock. Her left arm dangles by a strand of flesh that stretches like silly-putty, because her shoulder's been completely blown off. Jeff must have carved dum-dum crosses in his bullets.

I think, *I just bum-rushed a gun full of dum-dum bullets.* A cold flush mixes with my rising nausea.

There's a growing puddle around Natalie's feet like someone who's pissed themselves, except it's dark red, almost black in the dim light. She sits down in it, then lies down, breathing slower and slower.

When I look back at Jeff, he's still staring at her. Then he looks back at me, leans over and picks his gun up. I wait 'til he aims, watch the hammer 'til it leans back again, then I move faster than I ever have. I catch his wrist and twist, so the next dum-dum bullet goes off into the side of his head. I turn, stagger away from him, and puke in the middle of the floor. Once I collect myself, I dig out my cell phone and call the police. This woman took me back to her place to have sex. Her boyfriend was waiting to catch her cheating, and he turned the gun first on her, then on himself. Just like that crazy tattoo artist might have done, I think.

Down at the station, I fill out a statement. It takes all day for the case to open and shut. I don't know why Jeff didn't shoot me, I tell the cops, but I ain't complaining. The police take me home.

Once I'm alone, I remember the files in the back of Natalie's car. I wonder how deep the police will dig into Jeff and Natalie, and if I should think of getting scarce.

Probably not, but I sharpen for the possibility of the run, just in case.

Night falls, and I sleep like the dead in my nice, warm bed.

Island of Skulls

One

"We shall all dance the Dance of the Rising, in the House of Schrias, on the Island of Skulls." The husky voice sent an excited shiver down Ketz's spine.

One minute, he and his twin sister Tia were climbing the brambly, rocky hillside – a pair of lithe, nimble, wire-sculpture youths, with skin of swirling, earthen shades that blended with the forest-hues around them, better than any painted or woven camouflage could. They each wore leaf-wove vests and knee-length britches, with long knives and gear-pouches strapped to their sides. They'd spent all day chasing vague reports of unsavory activity in their territory, tracking from one side of the mountain to the other and back, sniffing for clues and questioning some hermitish outlying locals. Now here they were, back where they started, catching their breath, with nothing to show for it. High time they got back to the village, so they could wash up, then go kick back with some pals and a filched jug or two of Chief Lehirm's sap wine.

Then that strange girl had appeared over the ridge above, out of nowhere. She wasn't one of their own, that was for sure. Her thin skirt swirled and lashed about her hips, catching nebulous, kaleidoscopic patterns in the light, casting their splendors over the rocks and leaves. That was all she wore, except for the ominously carved coral jewelry that draped over her full breasts, wove about her slender wrists and between her supple, spidery fingers like gauntlets. Serpentine tattoos covered her smooth, ruddy skin. At a glance, you might miss how those were tattoos, that her flesh was naturally solid-shaded – not like that of the native Schomite of these hills.

Her lips lightly tickled Ketz's ear with the words – *We shall all dance the Dance of the Rising, in the House of Schrias, on the Island of Skulls* – then her fingernails brushed his cheek, before she danced away over the rocks. Her hair lashed about her shoulders as she glanced back. Her sultry gaze met his with hypnotic *Care to fuck?* eyes. He blinked, dizzy from her fragrance. His mouth watered. His fingers curled and uncurled, eager to explore her skin, to snarl through her wild, silken hair of gold and scarlet. A wisp of wind carried the scent away, as she darted downhill.

Tia sprang after the girl, even faster than Ketz did. She snatched at the lovely creature like some scrambling brush-rodent that might make a good dinner. Ketz bounded to catch up, to reach the girl before Tia did. Still the girl pranced away on bare feet, as though the sharp, prickly terrain couldn't touch her, like she was a ghost or something. Ketz knew she was no ghost. She felt and smelled too strong for that. She still evaded both him and Tia, before vanishing, laughing with that rich, red, wanton smile of hers.

Ketz caught up with Tia as the figure disappeared behind a large boulder. He dashed past his sister, rounded the rock, stopped and looked around. "Gone," he rasped. The late-day heat hung wet around his neck. "No tracks or scent or nothin', neither."

Tia slapped Ketz across the back of his head. "Maybe let the blood get back to your brain before you try more trackin'." She stalked past him, cocked her head and sniffed. Her pointy little ears twitched. "Huh, you're right. No sign of the little bitch, anywhere. Now how in the fuck...?"

"She said, *the Dance of the Rising, in the House of Schrias, on —*"

"I heard what she said," Tia snapped. She rolled her eyes. "*The Island of Skulls.* Ain't that around where the Ocro River flows into the Nagga River, near that one marsh village west of the Foothill Borders? Fuck, what's that town called again?"

"Pretty sure you mean Rothollow," said Ketz. "Anyhow, I figure it's time we get back to town. We need to go talk to Silisha."

Two

The Blend Lady's hut rested at the end of a short trail behind the village fellowship hall. A ratty cloth hung over her doorway, smelling of stale wine, sex, and magic. As the twins approached, more intoxicating aromas wafted out, from incense urns and pots on the stove within. Tia knocked on the frame.

A cheerful, lilting voice sounded from within, "Come on in, kids," as if Silisha knew to expect them.

STORY TIME WITH CRAZY UNCLE MATT

The twins shared an uneasily glance, then Tia pushed aside the curtain and stepped inside. The curtain fell back into place behind them, plunging them into shadows. A steamy, herb-scented mist settled over them. Their heads spun and their skin cooled, as the soothing energy of the Blend Lady's inner world enveloped them. It made them want to forget all the nasty realities of life outside, beyond the village, throughout the mountains, through all Deschemb. They couldn't do that, though. Those realities were why they were here.

Silisha stood by the stove, wearing only a light, loosely tied tan robe with the sleeves rolled up. Her dark, tangled hair hung clumped above her head in a messy bun, showing off her long neck. A gray, clay solution coated her arms, so she could handle the scalding chemicals in the pot without burning herself. She turned, beaming with both an ageless aura of wisdom and a flighty, girlish naivete. The solution she'd been blending dripped from her hands. "So sorry, I forgot to expect anyone." She came forward and hugged them both, leaving muddy smears on their backs and shoulders.

"No worries, really," said Ketz. As she drew away, his eyes kept trailing the ageless lady's curves. Tia elbowed him in the side.

Silisha pulled three stools to the center of the floor. She sat facing them, and waited for them to sit. "Funny to see you here, Ketz. Your next lesson's not 'til tomorrow."

"Uh, yeah, about that," said Ketz. "I might have to skip it."

Silisha frowned. "Might you, now."

"Yeah. There's been some weirdness in the woods today."

From a young age, their parents had tried foisting Tia on the Blend-Lady as a pupil, though the former had always gravitated towards more rambunctious pursuits. At seventeen, she and Ketz were already war-heroes to the Schomites of the Nagga Mountains. Ketz could damn sure fight, but he had more of the soul of a romantic dreamer. Out on the trail, Tia found herself having to look after his flighty ass because of it. At home in the village, he was the one drawn to Silisha's teachings. At times like this, that came in handy. He described his and Tia's encounter with the strange, dancing tattooed girl, on the forest ranges surrounding the village.

Silisha's face darkened as she pondered it. "*The Dance of the Rising*...on the Island of Skulls. Ketz, you say this strange young lady stopped to speak directly to you, at first sight?"

"Yeah," he said.

"More like suck his dick, practically," Tia muttered.

"That worries me most of all," said Silisha. She rose, turned away, and peered silently at some white-chalk scrawling across her back wall. "All these years, makin' something of myself here, for everything these these good mountains have given us...Now *they've* come back."

"If that message is a threat to you or anyone in this village, it's me and Tia's problem," said Ketz. "That's what we do."

Tia rolled her eyes, then said to Silisha, "You ever been out that way, downhill into those marshland villages?"

"*Been to them*...I remember them when they weren't even villages." When she turned back, her eyes were damp. She dried them and continued, "Back when I was young, when the Spirelight Empire drove our people into these hills, from all directions...I was just a student then. So was the young man my family took in with us, on the trail. His folks had been slaughtered by the Spirelight Police. My family took him in. Randish, we called him. Him and me, we took to one another fast. We were both learnin' together, about the mystical arts, anything any of the grown-ups found time to teach us. There wasn't much time to meditate proper on spiritual teachin's, on the trail, you know. Once things settled a little, guys and gals like him and me, we all had more time to find our own ways. Me and him, well...we were still learnin' from one another..." Her gaze drifted through bittersweet memories.

"We get it," said Tia. "You two was learnin' lots of old-world magic together. You was also fuckin'."

"So we were, since you wanna know." Silisha glared only a little. There were bigger concerns right now than Tia's insolence. "Some of the families on that trail, they settled those marshlands, learned how to farm kelp, got to trading with some other nearby vagabond settlements. That's what grew up into the village of Rothollow. There was an older Blend-Lady among us. Both Randish and me learned from her. Randish found somethin' else in those marshlands, though, somethin' he said he dreamed about. When he woke up from those dreams, he heard it callin' him from the murkier part of the river, somethin' long asleep. Our Blend-Lady felt it too, but she didn't like it. It didn't like her, either. She said she could tell.

"Before long, Randish stopped showin' up with me to her lessons. He'd just go straight to that spot by the river he liked so much, the place where he said he heard it speakin' to him strongest. He invited me to go there to listen with him. Our Blend-Lady advised me not to, but I did anyway.

I was young. I was in love. I was dumb.

"Whenever I went there with him, though...sure, I felt what he felt from that spot, but I never took to it like he did. I didn't like it at all. He was still okay, though, until the time he nearly drowned. He must'a just...waded out too far, to where he thought it was still shallow, but some undertow caught him and pulled him under. It was pure dumb luck, some tracker happened by that evening, saw him go under. By the time he got pulled out, he was drowned. Limp and dead as it gets. It was the Blend-Lady who managed to revive him. With her craft, she got the water out of his lungs, got the air back in him. When he woke up, though. he wasn't the same. He kept talkin' about what he found down there, about things long asleep, speakin' to him...somethin' that wanted more than communion and respect in exchange for natural power between realms. Didn't sound to me like any spirit of these lands, more like them glowin' gods the Spirelights worship. I didn't like what I heard, but the other kids did, the ones of the sensitive, mystical disposition, that is. After that, less and less of 'em went to see the Blend-Lady for guidance. Instead, they followed him to that spot by the river, to commune by night.

"I'd see their bonfires through the trees, heard the howling songs they sang. It got lonely around there, and scary. Randish didn't want nothin' of me, no more. I started seein' him around the village, with this other girl. She was arrogant and cruel...a Schomite for sure, but paler than any I'd seen so far north. Had all these weird tattoos on her skin..." Silisha's eyes settled on Ketz.

"Hey, wait," said Ketz. "You ain't sayin' you think...I mean, about that girl we met today..."

STORY TIME WITH CRAZY UNCLE MATT

Tia rolled her eyes. "No, Ketz, she ain't sayin' it was the same girl who was leadin' you around by the dick earlier. Hell, c'mon, that fancy little bitch was younger than us. Weren't for those tits hangin' off her, I'd be surprised if that soft-skinned little slut's bled yet."

"No, it couldn't be her," said Silisha. "That girl died."

"What, how?" the twins said in unison.

"She drowned in the flood, when the Spirelight Empire redirected the creek from the Western hills, so it washed out so much of those lowlands. They'd built a fellowship hall by then, up on a hill that got turned into an island by the flood, cut off from the rest of the town. Ever since, that fellowship hall's been left up there to rot, just an old ruin. For reasons none of us ever quite figured...a whole lot of the death caused by that flood, it all washed up on the banks of that island. The fallen trees, the dead critters, the dead people, all of it. No one can get out to that place without a boat, and no one felt like goin' near it, so all those corpses were just left to rot. On a hot day, you could smell it, too. That was the worst thing. To look at that island from the facing shore, you felt like all them corpses were starin' over back at you, out of all those rotten skulls. Someone called it the Island of Skulls, and it stuck.

"Anyhow, before all that happened...those other kids...I'd see 'em around with strange new cuts all over their bodies – not like they'd been scratched up in the brush or by some animal, but like they'd been carvin' on each other, puttin' the symbols on their own flesh, like they wanted to look like Randish's new girl, with all her tattoos. Little by little, I stopped seein' some of the kids around at all. The ones who broke from that group, said they didn't like what they found...all those kids just washed up on the riverbank, too long-drowned for any Blend-Lady to bring 'em back. Not that I could find my Blend-Lady anymore, either. Eventually, someone dragged her corpse out of the river, too.

"Then the flood happened. My folks saw it comin', got to higher ground in time. Not long afterwards, they decided it was time to move on, like all reasonable folks. We found our way up into these hills. Randish was one of those who stayed behind, with his family, in those waterlogged lands. Don't ask me how, but they somehow grew the town of Rothollow on that desolate, soggy, accursed land. I ain't heard hide nor hair of him since, but every now and then, I catch some word from stray travelers, about Rothollow. They always mention the *Island of Skulls*. I hear about mystics in silken green coats, in places where one doesn't normally see such finery as that.

"I'd about forgotten those days, until the last few nights. 'Cause I always watch the stars. And I always mind my dreams. Now you two come to me with this news, and it's all come back...everything *he* used to talk about...now as the Full Red Moon rises into the configuration of constellations called the House of Schrias, the time of the Dance of the Rising...Makes sense, I guess, this should all come now."

"How's that?" asked Tia.

"Since the fall of the Spirelight City State of Trescha, since their Empire's grip has loosened from our people in these surrounding lands, during their own times of chaos...Old magic long denied has drawn once more to the people, called to us all. Some of it's good. Some of it's bad. Whatever this is from Rothollow, it's bad. In all that time, much that's been buried has gone mad, gone rotten where it lies, like I felt back then, from the marshlands. Back then, that flood came, sorted it all out. Now here comes the prancing nymph again, drawin' sweet, dear Ketz, as it drew my Randish, towards the waters to the west. The winds have blown those fetid scents uphill, to me. You say you've both been to that marsh village before?"

Tia thumbed at Ketz. "Pa used to take him there when we were younger. Never took me. I've only been out that way a couple times, in later years. Best I can figure, the Spirelight Empire ain't bothered those fuckers, just 'cause both them *and* their lands are so ass-fuck nasty, the Empire just leaves 'em the hell alone. Hell, just thinkin' about those marshes puts the stench back in my nose."

Ketz mulled it over. "That weird girl, the one who brought the news...Wherever she fits into all this, seems pretty obvious she wanted us to know. Like maybe she agrees with us, that it needs to be stopped."

"Maybe," said Tia. "Or maybe it's a trap."

"Either way, Ketz, honey..." Silisha cracked a rye smile at him. "Listen to your sister on this one: don't go into this thinkin' with your dick."

Three

After their talk with Silisha, the twins went home and slept for the evening. They struck out at dawn for Rothollow. The journey took two days, over terrain that left even their spry legs cramped. They made camp in a glade a few miles out, took a day there to recuperate, get themselves sharp, then reach the village just in time for the moon to rise into the House of Schrias. They left their supplies in the glade, everything but the long, curved, jagged knives on their belts.

Now the red moon rose over the soggy foothills. All around, peepers shrieked in agitation. Tia and Ketz descended the thickly wooded hillside, towards the few blinking windows. Ahead, there spread the marshland village of Rothollow, a nestled hovel of structures that rose on stilts between a network of swaying walkways where kelp-farmers toiled by day. Beyond that, the the river shimmered, mingling with the dancing flames that glowed from within the old walls, out on the Island of Skulls.

Since the flood, the people here had devolved into a bent, twisted, insular, inbred lot, distrustful and spiteful of outsiders, save for a few neighboring bandit gangs, who sometimes called on them for bloodthirsty alliances that promised ample plunder. That's where Tia and Ketz came in. Ketz had ventured here to recruit them for the sacking of Trescha. Normally, that would be an advantage. Tonight, though, the drumbeat echoed out from that island, a sound full of frenzied malice, awaiting what the moon would bring.

All the while, the strange forest girl's nimble shape danced through Ketz's mind. Her lush scent and wanton red smile taunted him onward. Right as he started getting a stiffy, Tia elbowed him in the side. "Hey, you. Get your game-face on."

"Don't worry." He thumbed the pommel of his knife. "I'm all set for this shit."

"That's what worries me," she muttered.

Through the brush ahead, the first bridge led off onto the network of suspended walkways. To their left, two figures emerged from a narrow, shrouded trail – stealthy scouts like themselves, though of this town. They went right past Tia and Ketz without noticing them. The twins followed silently, onto the suspended wooden walkways that ran between all the dim muck-and-twig dwellings. These marshland scouts all wore strange, mismatched assemblies of leather armor, from all eight winds of Deschemb, collected from raided caravans over the years, tied on haphazardly over the same rags worn by the civilian locals.

Neither Tia nor Ketz had ever cared for armor. On the one hand, their bodies showed it, with scars from wounds no civilized man or woman would survive, let alone so young. Still, they moved freer and deadlier when unencumbered...and quieter, like now.

Ahead, the two scouts met up with a third man, clearly their commander. "Quiet all around out there," said one of them, shivering and hugging himself, "considerin' all that lizardshit out there over the water."

"Oh, what, 'cause of the Nagga's Bride?" said the other. "Nah, with all that trouble Bossman Randish has stirred up, his dick all hard for that infernal slut...Anyone with sense knows to stay clear tonight...friend or foe."

"Fuck it, you're right," said the leader. "C'mon, boys, let's go chug some grog."

They headed to a crossroad, by which rose a larger hut, more brightly lit than the others. That was the village tavern, Ketz recalled. As he and Tia crept closer to the scouts, he recognized the leader. He had no love for these local boys, but they were all veteran allies to the Schomites of the Nagga Mountains. Still, it seemed best to feel things out more, before revealing themselves to anyone, especially with everyone on edge over strange rumors.

Tia's foot slid and scraped the crooked walkway boards. The scouts all spun, peering through the murk. Their jagged, curved blades chimed free and pointed at the gloom. The leader stepped to the fore, went *en garde*, and snarled, "Who's that out there?"

Ketz lifted his hands and stepped into the dim light of the tavern windows. "Easy there, man. Just a couple of scouts like you."

"*Scouts*, my ass." The leader squinted. "Look more like a couple half-naked feral-brats to me. C'mon, speak up. Step into the light, slow-like or I'll...Hey, hold up. That Ketz?"

"Howdy, Claid."

Claid sheathed his blade and motioned his companions to do the same. In the next instant, he lunged forward and caught Ketz in a violent embrace. "Well, I'll be fucked by a spine-rat! What the hell you doin' here, man? Hey, is that your pretty sister you got with you? How you doin', beautiful? Missed me?"

"Yeah, it's me, and no, I ain't." Tia stepped into the light next to Ketz. Her palm stayed on her knife. "Keep your voices down, all of you. We ain't supposed to be here."

"The fuck you talkin' about?" said Claid. "You two know you're always welcome here, far as I'm concerned. Hey, *Trescha for life*, right?"

"*Trescha for life*," said Ketz.

"Sure," said Tia. "Keep it down, all the same."

Claid's companions snickered between them. One of them said, "Hear that, Claid? Sounds like this little highland bitch is tryin' to give you orders!"

"She's givin' me advice, is what she's doin'," Claid snarled over his shoulder at them. "*I'm* givin' you boys orders, to shut the fuck up."

"Yeah, but —"

"You heard me. Both of y'all, get on inside. Get me a tankard. I'll be along directly." Once they were gone, he whispered, "Sorry everyone's so jumpy, guys. It's a weird night 'round here...a *bad* night."

"We know," said Ketz. "That's why we're here."

"Yeah," said Tia. "From what we just heard, sounds like it's your own town boss creatin' that disturbance. I don't see none of you boys doin' fuckall about it."

"Right, well, 'cause...he's the bossman." Claid lowered his eyes. "I'm sworn to my post here, under his authority, like them boys you just saw are sworn under mine."

"Oh, right, I almost forgot," said Tia. "You Rothollow boys still hold to all that *sworn sacred allegiance, right or wrong* lizardshit."

"Careful there, girly." Claid stepped in close and loomed over Tia. "You're in Rothollow, not the Nagga Mountains."

Ketz spotted the glimmer in Tia's eyes, the subtle shift in her shoulders. Veteran of Trescha or not, Claid had no idea how close he was to eating his own testicles. Ketz stepped between them and got nose to nose with Claid. "Yeah, and your bossman's all in with some *Nagga's Bride*. Sure sounds like Nagga Mountain business to me, huh, sis?"

"How much was you two listenin' in on?" said Claid.

"Enough," said Tia. "Some of you marshlanders' weirdness has crept up into our hills. We don't like the smell of it. So we came to make sure it's nothin' bodes ill for these here surrounding parts. From the sound of things, it don't bode so well for y'all, either. What's happenin' over on the Island of Skulls?"

"Some big ceremony goin' down. Don't ask me what it's all about. I don't know."

"Got somethin' to do with your bossman's old girlfriend showin' back up?" said Tia.

Claid blanched. "*Old* girlfriend? I don't know what you two been hearin' up in your hills, but...'tween us, it's fuckin' gross, seein' 'em around, carryin' on in public like they do. But who's gonna say shit 'bout the town boss's business, with how things have gotten since she showed up...not so long after we all got home from Trescha, come to think of it. Randish wasn't the town boss then. I got home, the old bossman had just died. Randish was just then makin' his bid for it. Funny, he never before struck me as the type, such a docile old fat fuck and all. Soon as he took up with that lil' gal, though...It was weird, everyone who opposed him just started dyin'. Or worse, if they had kids, or old folks they was takin' care of, it was those weak ones who'd turn up dead. And not like they'd go missin', neither. Like those folks who opposed the town boss or his demon-slut gal, their youngsters or elders would go to sleep safe and warm, then their loving guardians would wake up the next morning and find their beds empty. Then not long after, the corpses would wash up somewhere on the riverbanks. People say that gal of his just *walked right out of the river* one day. By now, I sorta believe it. Now, tonight, they's all out on that island, in that rotten old fellowship hall."

"Who?" said the twins in unison.

"What townsfolk took to those two like flies on shit,

that's who. Not the folks who bowed before 'em 'cause they was scared, 'cause they didn't want no more of their loved ones to disappear and wash up dead. I mean the *real* zealous ones, the ones who really bought into what the bossman's new lady promised 'em, all the long-buried riches from the depths." Claid turned to the side and spat. "Funny, I ain't seen none of even them folks reapin' such riches. That's what's given everyone back here in town the jitters...what real riches those zealots are out to raise from them depths themselves...what we all feel in the air tonight...what they just might bring back with 'em."

"Who do they got over there for security?" said Tia, glowering.

"None of my boys, thank the lands," said Claid. "The ones they keep as their personal security wandered in from the northeastern hills. They look and smell like death, like someone really *did* haul 'em out of some watery grave for this job. I don't know where they come from. All day, they been rowin' them's of Randish's inner circle over there, on flatboats. Must be a few dozen of 'em gathered out there by now. What do you two aim to do about it?"

"Well, hearin' you talk about it," said Tia, "I kinda wanna get over there and kill every last one of those cocksuckers." She side-eyed her brother. "Ketz?"

"I'm more up to play it by ear," said Ketz. "But...yeah, let's get on over there."

Claid mulled it over sullenly. "Y'all realize, if you fail at this and word gets out I helped you, I'm dead. So's my gal and the brat in her belly."

"You don't help us," said Tia, "it might not matter."

"Yeah? So what if I do? Word gets out you two came here to kill fellow Schomites, there'll be fresh feuds 'tween the marshlands and the Nagga Mountains. Divided like that, we'll be ripe for the Spirelight Empire to swarm in and take all our asses out."

"Hey, Claid," said Tia, "you're smarter than I figured. That ain't sayin' much, but still."

"We'll get the job done, in and out real quiet-like," said Ketz. "That's what we do."

Claid scowled and sighed. "You'll need to get across that river. There's a little dock no one goes to no more. I'll show you to it. There's a little boat you can take across."

"Thank you," said Ketz.

Tia said to Claid, "If this turns out to be a trap, I'm gonna fuck you in the ass with your own severed cock, if it's the last thing I do. Anyhow, lead the way, stud."

Four

Claid led them along a narrow, slippery trail. To the right, a steep slope dropped down to the river. To the left, the hillside rose just as steeply, jutting with brambles and branches and vines that kept smacking them in the face.

Tia brushed wet leaves from her face and spat bits of them out of her mouth. "What asshole decided to keep a boat someplace you have to get to like this?"

"Quiet," hissed Claid, crouching. "Some asshole smart enough to stake a kelp an' fish claim where it's too big a pain in the ass for anyone else to poach on, that's who. By the way, girly, that smart asshole's me. There it is, right up ahead." He pointed.

They could see it ahead, just downhill from the next

bend, through the branches. The red moon rippled off the waves and the sandy bank. Claid hurried towards it. Tia and Ketz followed. To their relief, the path widened underfoot as the foliage cleared. Then they froze. Two figures stood on the bank, flanking the spike that tethered the bobbing boat. They stood armored in vests and gauntlets and greaves of burnt-black bone, over matching britches, tunics and boots that looked too clean and refined for all this whispering rot around them. In their fists, they clutched great spears of flame-hardened shafts and long, jagged-edged blades.

Ketz whispered to Tia, "Who the fuck are those –"

Claid was already dashing down the ridge, right at the bastards. He ripped his blade out mid-stride and brandished it at them. "Hey! *Hey!* What you boys think you're doin' out here, huh? This is my fuckin' claim, *mine!* Go on, *git!*"

"Great," hissed Tia, "just fuckin' great." She and Ketz hurried downhill after him.

The men converged and pointed their spears at Claid. "It's the Nagga's Bride's claim, like everything in Rothollow now belongs to the Nagga's Bride," said one of them.

"Don't you get that yet, boy?" said the other, tickling Claid's chest with the spear's tip. "You've been workin' this claim for *her*. You just ain't declared it to her yet, like you should. So here we are, to make sure you –"

Claid growled and lunged in at them. He bobbed under the spears as they fanned in at him, their weapons unfit for such unexpected close quarters. He rose between them and bashed one in the face with the butt of his knife. The man staggered away, the shaft flailing in one hand, while his other palm clutched at his shattered, blood-spurting nose.

The other man had sense enough to drop his spear and draw his short knife, fixing to jab Claid in the back. Tia slipped up behind the guy and slashed his throat. Ketz bounded past her, splashing through the surf up to Claid's side. Together, Ketz and Claid stared down their remaining enemy. The man had splashed backwards, knee-deep into the water, but he'd recovered his senses by now. He crouched with the seasoned poise of a veteran fighter, glaring murderously. With one iron-muscled arm, he thrust out his spear. His other hand had drawn his dagger, held overhead like a scorpion's stinger. Ketz and Claid exchanged quick, tense glances, then stared at the spearman. One way or the other, in the next second or two, at least one of these three men would be dead.

Far behind the spearman, high atop a mossy ridge, a silver laugh chimed through the night. "So comes our witness from the Nagga Mountains," she called. Her eyes glowed in the night, while the red moon spilled curious patterns through the branches, across her soft, swaying, nearly naked shape. She lifted one bejeweled hand and wiggled her fingers at Ketz. Even from here, he caught her musky scent. His brain swam and his mouth watered. In the same instant, she dove off the hillside, splashed and vanished beneath the surface of the river.

Something else splashed, much closer to Ketz. The spearman had lunged forward. Claid gulped and folded forward as the shaft drove through his abdomen. The spearman kept coming, thrusting the spear so hard that it busted through the center of Claid's back and sent bloody chips of spine flying everywhere. The man bore down on Ketz, his dagger flashing as it descended. Ketz braced his sinking feet and hacked upwards. The attacker's arm split at the elbow. A forearm and knife flew away and landed on the shore somewhere. The man howled and reeled backwards. His pruned arm flailed, showering blood across both Ketz and the water's surface. Ketz roared and sprang, tackling the fucker. They splashed and floundered in the surf together. Ketz stayed on top, straddling the other. He shoved the twisting, shaking face underwater and held it there. His knife rose and fell, shattering the armor then gouging the neck and torso over and over, 'til the body sunk heavier from the drunk-up river and stopped coughing out bubbles. Ketz kept stabbing.

"Ketz...*Ketz!*" It was Tia. She grabbed his shoulder.

He almost elbowed her in the face before he came to his senses. He rose panting and growling from the waves. The water felt soupy and hot around him from all the blood. Tia still gripped his shoulder.

A groan sounded behind them, so they both turned. *"Oh, shit...Ooooh, shit, man! Fuuuck!"* Claid lay twisted on his side on the bank. His limp legs bobbed in the water like dead fish. Blood leaked from his front and back, making a dark cloud in the water around his groin, like someone pissing blood. He kept pulling at the shaft through his body, which just increased the agony, so he kept sobbing, *"Fuuuuuuuck!"*

The sight and sound of it had to be the most horrific thing the twins had ever heard in their young lives. They hurried over and knelt on either side of him.

"Hey, man, easy there," said Ketz. He guided Claid's bloody hands away from the spear. "Stop hurtin' yourself like that! *Hey!* Hey, c'mon, now."

Claid's hands gripped Ketz's hard enough to hurt. He grinned up. "Hey! Hey, Ketz! What the fuck you doin' here in Rothollow, huh? Say, you bring that pretty sister of yours with – Aw, *fuuuuck*, man, this hurts!"

Tia settled and rested Claid's head in her lap. "I'm right here, you asshole."

Ketz met her eyes pleadingly. She looked Claid over, looked back up at her brother, and shook her head. He gritted his teeth and nodded.

Claid's eyes rolled around at them. "Oh, fuck yeah, am I right? *Trescha for life*, huh?"

Ketz grinned through his tears, squeezing Claid's fist. "That's right, buddy. Fuck yeah. *Trescha for life.*"

"Trescha for life, Claid," said Tia. She stroked his cheek, kissed his forehead, then jammed her knife into his brain, through his ear. He jerked, then slumped still.

Ketz said numbly, "Back in town, he said he had a girl with a brat in her belly. He never told me about her."

Tie shrugged. "Didn't stop him from hittin' on me, did it now?" She yanked her knife out of Claid's skull, shoved him out of her lap, and stood up. Claid's dead hands still clung stiffly to Ketz. He pried the fingers away, stood up, and splashed out of the water after his sister. She crouched next to the first of the two enemy corpses, the one on dry land that she'd killed. Ketz crouched on the other side of it. They examined it together. Claid hadn't lied. Those guys weren't from around here. By this one's swirly gray-and-green skin, they might be Wallutians.

"Where the hell you figure this bossman's recruitin' these fuckers from?" said Ketz.

Tia glared over his shoulder, at the hillside beyond, where the spectral near-naked beauty had stood moments ago. "Don't you mean *where's your new girlfriend recruitin' 'em from?*"

Ketz followed her gaze to the spot. He snarled, rose, and headed for the boat. "What's it matter? Let's get across the river and kill 'em all."

"Including her, right?" said Tia.

Ketz didn't answer.

Five

The river was calm on the surface, at least enough so they made the little boat glide smooth and straight across it.

All the way over, some hot malevolence brewed beneath them in the bobbing current, like an otherworldly infection rising from the water. It set their nerves tingling. The big, bloody moon grinned down at them, ever brighter, coasting through the black firmament towards the midnight hour, right above the old fellowship hall.

The boat glided in across wavering scum and water-weeds, 'til the stern drove into wet sand. Along the shore, to the left and right, there rested half a dozen tethered flatboats. Tia and Ketz climbed out onto the shore. Their blades slid silently from the scabbards. They crept uphill, weaving between the twisting dead trees and old bones. Sometimes they moved in single-file, sometimes side by side. They let their feet feel out and navigate the treacherous ground. Several times, their feet sank through old skeletons, which broke beneath them like rotted twigs.

The higher they climbed, the fuller they saw the building. Through the windows and open doorway, torches hung ablaze from the walls. Two or three dozen celebrants squirmed and writhed about, in anticipation of whatever

Bossman Randish had promised them. A darkened stage rose at the back of the great hall. It fell off on either side, into shadowy hindquarters.

Tia and Ketz crept towards a window for a better look. They paused and hung back in the shadowy foliage. Two sentries flanked the main door, armored like the ones they'd faced on the opposite bank. The twins stalked around through the outer brush, and darted down the left side of the building. There they expected to find a rear entrance, as per the general layout of structures like this, which they did. Two more bone-clad sentries flanked the rear side door. Tia and Ketz exchanged nods and fanned out. From either side, they got within a few feet of the men. A bar of light passed over Tia's head, through the last window under which she crept. Both watchmen spotted her. They shifted sharply, aiming their spears her way.

She jumped out into the light and yanked open her vest. *"Hey, boys, look at my tits!"*

While they obliged, she sprang at them. That trick never failed. Her gleaming blade flashed for their vitals. As they lunged at her, Ketz sprang in behind the one closest to him. He locked his arm around the bastard's neck and jammed his knife in beneath the armor, through the lower side, into the kidney. His palm clamped over the man's mouth. Black blood gushed out over his knife-hand. The man's dying thrashes brought his companion up sharp. That gave Tia just enough time to close in on him, past his spear. She grabbed the shaft and yanked him sideways, off balance. She looked him straight in the eyes while she drove her knife through his chest-plate, into his heart. At least he died seeing something pretty.

Tia and Ketz caught the sinking, shuddering corpses

and lowered them silently to the ground. They then darted through the side door, into the long, dark hallway. On the way, Tia pulled her vest shut. In here, the infernal drumbeat pulsed through the walls, from the floorboards. Its sweetly malicious rhythms pulsed up through their bodies. They came to the end of the hallway, hung back, and peered out over the edge of the stage from behind a jutting partition. A great, jagged hole spread across the rotting, arching ceiling, spilling red moonlight across the altar at the center of the stage. It grew brighter as the moon drifted towards its zenith.

Out in the main hall, to left and right, the drummers lined the walls, perched on perforated iron platforms. They tattooed out a brain-shaking harmony, to which the celebrants hopped and squirmed and capered, colliding and rubbing against each other ecstatically. Something was strange – just plain damn wrong – about the drummers. At first, in the uneven light, neither of the twins could tell what. Then their eyes adjusted, and they looked at each other, just to make sure neither was hallucinating. The drums were made of great metal tubes, fused to the platforms, out of which the sound echoed. At first, it looked like withered, nearly skeletal bodies lay on their backs in front of each tube. No, those bodies lay *around* the tubes. The corpses had been hollowed out from behind, their spines removed, with their abdominal flesh stretched all the way to the floor, creating a smooth surface at the top around the rims of the cylinders, on which the naked drummers' palms danced. Each flesh-tube was wrapped in a braid of spiked wire, holding the drummers in place. The drummers' eyes all stared glassy and dead, out at the dancers. Most of the dancers out on the floor were naked or close enough, covered in blood, mud, river-slime, and who knew what else.

"Where the hell's this Bossman Randish everyone keeps talkin' about?" Tia hissed.

Ketz perked up and sniffed the fetid air. "Oh, he's around."

"How do you know so much, all of a sudden?"

"Because so does *she*. The one who wanted us here."

"Oh, forfucksake," said Tia. "I thought we agreed, no thinkin' with your dick."

"That ain't what this is, I promise."

"Oh yeah? So what's your bright idea?"

"They're both around here somewhere. Bossman Randish and...that girl. They're waitin' for just the right moment to make their grand entrance. I can feel it. Just look at that crowd out there. They'll be on the stage, soon, together. The true *Dance of the Rising* is about to start. They're waitin' 'til the moon's just right, in the House of Schrias. We can't let 'em come together beneath that spill of moonlight, Tia. We can't."

"Fine. So what *can* we do?"

"You take crowd control. I'll take backstage."

"Works for me, 'cept what do you expect to...?"

"This is an instinct I'm followin', through the rhythm of these lands."

"These lands - this island - are fucking poison!"

"Exactly. Just, c'mon, sis, trust me for once. All you gotta do is get out there, mingle with the dance, and be ready to kill a bunch of motherfuckers any second now."

Tia glanced out at the grotesque celebrants. Some of the guys and gals out there didn't look half-bad, all things considered, at least for Rothollow folk. "Okay, since you put it that way...Hell, I done worse." She grinned and licked her lips.

With that, she darted up behind the partition, hopped down between it and the stage, and slipped out into the crowd. Through the broken overhead ceiling, she saw Deschemb's red moon rising to its zenith...into the center of the broken opening, shining on the stage, from the House of Schrias. In the rising, frenzied heat of anticipation, the congregation squirmed around her.

As the rhythm moved through her, a weird thing happened. The collective stench no longer bothered her. The rhythmic buzz through her body took on an invigorating, rotten-fruit sweetness. Before she knew it, she wasn't *pretending* to dance with these degenerates. She *was* dancing with them. She threw herself into it, thrashing and twisting and arching herself about. Other dancers landed against her and moaned at her warmth. She shoved some of them away, writhed and gyrated against others. Outside, something echoed from the river, boiling ever closer through the sweltering essence of the night. Whatever it was, it was still ephemeral. It hadn't risen from the depths, wasn't *physically* closing in around this building – around the whole world – yet.

The drummers stopped. The dancers went still. They all stared forward as one, up at the stage. Tia followed their gaze, then she looked out through the windows on either side. She spotted her brother emerging onto the stage.

"Oh, *sonofabitch*," she muttered.

Six

Ketz maneuvered silently through the blackness backstage. His sharp eyes adjusted to the gloom easily enough, but it was his nose he followed now, ever closer to the same otherworldly fragrance he hadn't been able to shake since she'd first whispered in his ear.

Save your adrenaline-boner for the celebration afterwards, Ketz. What celebration? He was on his way to kill her, and Claid was dead. The sooner he and Tia put Rothollow behind them, the better.

From outside, the hot rumbling beneath the waves thundered through his being...through his bloodstream, eager to be born. As he crept towards the true source, he forgot everything else. It was all he'd been able to do, to hold himself back, to stay calm, to assess and calculate, like on any other job.

As the drums fell silent, he reached the opposite stage entrance. From the gloom of the back wall, two figures stepped forward, into the red light that spilled in onto the stage, from the night outside. The first was a man, tall and proud-shouldered. He looked about Silisha's age, but hadn't aged as well. He'd sure dandied himself up to hide it, though! His hair was slicked-back and oily, and he wore a silken, dark-green coat that hung to the floor, over clean black trousers and shoes. His patchy, mold-infected face and yellowy, bloodshot eyes were purely of the marshland Schomites, though, all the more grotesque for the buzzing madness of his zealotry, worse still for the very real powers that fueled his madness, from the red night.

Ketz stepped out into the light of the stage. He no

longer kept quiet. The man in the green coat drew up sharp and turned to face him. So did the other figure. She spread her arms wide, jingling her coral jewelry. Her eyes met Ketz's. Her sweet scent burned through all the rot.

The green-coated man didn't look surprised at all. "Ah, and what have we here? This, my dear, must be the witness from the Nagga Mountains you promised...a student of dear Silisha, yes, I smell it on him."

Ketz glared. "You must be ol' Bossman Randish, huh?"

"*Bossman*, you call me?" Randish strode forward. His his dark, beady eyes flashed hypnotically. He laughed haughtily. "Ah, yes, they'll call me that for a little while longer. Once what we raise here tonight envelopes them, those who survive will call me *Priest King Randish.*"

The strange, elusive beauty stepped up between them. She draped her long arms on both their shoulders. "I take it you're pleased, m'lord," she said, batting her eyelashes.

"Well, he's younger than I expected...but we'll make do with him just fine, won't we?"

"Oh no, m'lord," she said. Her palm ran up and down Ketz's side, raising goose-flesh all over him. "Not us...but oh, how *I* look forward to *making do* with him."

Randish looked at her sharply. "Wait, what do you —"

Her hand fastened on the knife on Ketz's belt, ripped it from the scabbard, and planted it deep in Bossman Randish's neck. Randish stared at her as his eyes went glassy. With a sweet smile, she jerked the knife free with such force that his whole neck split wide open and his head yawned back, clinging on by the spine. A crimson spray showered the girl, Ketz, and those in the crowd closest to the foot of the stage. Randish's corpse crashed to the boards, where it sprawled and shuddered.

Ketz couldn't hear anyone or anything out in the hall...not as though the crowd had gone silent, more like they just weren't there anymore, like some black void had swallowed them. He still heard the river rushing and rising somewhere, but that was all. He and the girl stood face to face. His hands ran up and down her arms, 'til he found her still clutching his dripping knife. He pried it from her, cast it aside, then caught her in his arms and pulled her close. She writhed against him, as their flesh heated up together, then she reached down, stroked and gripped him through his trousers.

Sweet fuck, if she didn't slow down with that, he'd be done before they even started! His trembling hand guided hers away from his crotch. Then his other hand tore off her skirt, found her bare beneath it, played with her between the legs, driving her wild so her thighs yawned open. He pressed her down onto the boards, even as the blood of her slain master spread out around them. They slipped and slid through it together. He fondled her, sucked on her, twisted out of his trousers, shoved his stiffening cock into her, then went insane, fucking her hard.

They weren't on stage anymore. They were underwater together, in the boiling river. Things that had slept down there for ages rose around them, moaning and gurgling delight at their union. He thrust harder and deeper, bit at her, gnawed on her, pinched her nipples, gripped her thighs, forcing them as far apart as they'd go, unable to get enough of her. She tightened her thighs around him and pressed his chest so he swayed back. She rose up over him, put him on his back, and rode him. She arched her chest out, slung her hair around, caressed herself all over, staring down into his eyes.

Nearby, people were shrieking. A lot of people. What was with them? It was the congregation in the fellowship hall, bustling to life again, not dancing this time, instead trampling each other to get away, smacking into each other with sickening meat-packing thuds. Why? He couldn't tell. What did it matter? All that was far away. His dark goddess had him.

"Mmmmm, yes, Ketz," the Goddess purred in his ear. "Feel it close, baby? Yeah, *this* is what happens at the Dance of the Rising in the House of Schrias. I knew, all I was missing was the cock of the Nagga Mountains. It's *us*, baby, fucking the whole world!"

"Ketz...Ketz!"

His sister's voice echoed to him through the murky distance. What the hell did she want? Couldn't she tell he was busy?

"Ketz!"

He was close to the end, wanted to keep this going for as long as he could...longer...forever. He grabbed the goddess's ass, tried to steady her rocking so she didn't make him blow his load so quick, but she just rode him harder and harder, until...

Something struck him on the side of the head, the edge of someone's palm. He blinked, His vision cleared. He stared up at the girl he'd come here for, the siren he'd claimed and conquered...

His eyes cleared some more. That wasn't a goddess. It wasn't a siren, either. Her neck and limbs and fingers had grown monstrously long, like wild willow branches covering the whole stage, splitting off and snaking out into the hall beyond. All the windows had shattered, so the massive, slithering, half-glimpsed shapes outside snaked in, to meet and join with her...with him...with them both.

There was his knife, hovering above her – above *it* – in the air, the one she'd taken from him to kill her used-up acolyte. No, not his knife. Tia's knife, in Tia's hand, her purple eyes flashing, her pretty face twisted into a feral hellcat snarl. She drove the blade in and out of the body that writhed over Ketz, so it squirted blood all over her face and neck.

All the torches had gone out. Outside, a thick, black cloud had passed over the moon, extinguishing the red spill. Something sopping and cold swayed heavily over Ketz. Through the hole in the ceiling, the moon came back into view. It now gleamed pale and clean. He still had his dick stuck in a rotting corpse, a putrid cadaver that had lain stagnating in the swamp for all the years since the flood. It oozed black blood from all the gashes Tia's blade had made. Ketz's guts rolled. He shoved the leaky corpse so it slid off and tumbled sideways with a wet plop. Shuddering, he scrambled backwards across the boards, wiping frantically at the slime on his junk before hopping to his feet and jerking his trousers up.

His head cleared, his breathing settled, and he looked around. No one remained in the hall except the dead guys who'd been turned into drums, plus some celebrants who'd been trampled to death while the others fled.

Tia stood in the spill of moonlight, next to the two corpses on the stage. She found Ketz's knife, picked it up, wiped it off and held it out to him. "You might not wanna forget this."

"Thanks." He took it numbly and sheathed it. "What the fuck was all that?"

"Whatever these sick bastards were out to raise from the deeps...you raised it. You and your girlfriend there. Guess now we know why they wanted you here for it."

"Holy shit, you mean...that was all real? All those...tentacles and shit?"

"Yeah. Anyway, it's dead now. So's anyone who knew how to poke it back to life. Hopefully it got most of the congregation who managed to run out screaming. Don't figure they'll be a problem for Rothollow no more, anyhow. 'Least you didn't get to, uh, finish. Whatever those demons, monsters, things were, I don't wanna know what they'd'a meant for the whole countryside." She looked him over. Her face twisted in disgust, then softened. "Hey. You okay there?"

"No. Heh, yeah, sure, I will be, after a good long wash in the mountain stream once we get home. Hey...uh...thanks, by the way."

"Don't mention it," said Tia. "No, really, don't. Matter of fact, let's never talk about this night again."

The Reverend

No one knew exactly when the Reverend started traveling with us. He disappeared sometime while we were camped out on the old farmer's land.

This all happened a long time ago, sometime back in the 1960's. I spent years just assuming most of the folks from our old caravan were dead by now. Then Facebook came along, and everyone started reconnecting through friends of friends and such. Next thing I knew, I was staying up late, getting into long, deep conversations with people I'd almost forgotten existed. It was only a matter of time, before we finally talked about the Reverend.

These modern times, I tell you. Everything's under the microscope on the damned Internet, and all I hear is that booming voice declaring, *"And the Lord shall bring every work into judgment, with every secret thing, whether it be good, or whether it be evil."*

The Reverend's long gone by now. So is Doc Campbell. The Internet's the new god that brings every secret thing back into the light, into judgment. Judgment is usually a lazy substitute for puzzling out the truth. I suspect the Reverend would agree. The truth's always more confusing, and a lot scarier.

Everyone first saw the Reverend at some roadside rest stop, just talking to whoever struck up a conversation with him. No one agrees which state that rest stop was in. When we got back on the road, he came with us. He must have climbed onto the old bus, or into someone's van or car. Right, just asked if he could hitch a lift a few towns over or something. Next thing anyone knew, he made himself right at home with us, on the road. Him and the old dog that followed him everywhere. He called the dog Providence. Providence was a smelly, friendly, panting, mangy old beast that could be trying when it wanted your affection, but it never snapped or barked at anyone.

None of the girls claimed to be have been fucking the Reverend. Sure, plenty of them wanted to. Who could blame them? Even I have to admit, he was a good ol' fashioned drop-dead handsome beast of a man, tall and straight-backed with a clean-shaven V-shaped granite face. Even his black clothes couldn't tame his broad, powerful shoulders, his silky swept-back black hair, or those pale, piercing eyes beneath the wide-brimmed black hat. Heaven and hell rumbled like distant thunder through his voice. He carried only a small, tan leather suitcase with a few changes of clothes in it. He carried his Bible in his breast pocket next to his heart. Actually, I don't think that book was the Bible, but I'll get to that.

Anyway, no, the girls all claimed, the most the Reverend ever did was a little coy flirting. His whole presence and manner were like nothing anyone of our generation had seen, except in black-and-white-faded-to-tan photographs from at least two generations ago, sitting on someone's mantle back home, even those of us who'd run away from strict, old-fashioned religious families. No one could figure out how old he was. An ancient, primordial aura surrounded him, though physically, he looked no older than the eldest in our caravan. And these were the days when you weren't supposed to trust anyone over thirty, remember.

So what the hell was an old-fashioned man of God doing, tagging along with our free-loving, free-wheeling, drug-smoking heathen band? To save souls and guide our wayward generation back into the fold? No, he'd never once tried that with any of us either...not exactly. In a way, though, looking back, that's exactly what he did, in his own way.

The old farmer's land lay on the hilly, darkly wooded outskirts of Sturgeon, Vermont, about an hour north of the Massachusetts border. We were supposedly headed for a commune a lot further north, but we were low on gas and money. We had to stop somewhere, for a while, to accumulate more of both, somehow. I'd pointed out Sturgeon on the map and said I had family there, folks with a big place, who'd take us in. When we got there, though, my aunt and uncle turned us away. They didn't like the state I'd come to, or the company I'd taken up with.

So there we were in Sturgeon. While the rest of us asked each other "What now?", the Reverend wandered out to the hillside many yards from the road. He stood there for a while like a rugged, regal statue, as though speaking silently with his Lord in the late afternoon sun. Finally he cocked his chin up, called some of us over, and pointed out the farmhouse in the distance across the rolling hills. Why not, we all figured. Sure, we'd go knock on their door. It was as good a thing to try as any.

Once we found our way there, Doc Campbell insisted on going to talk to the residents first. He only grudgingly agreed to let the Reverend go with him. The rest of us waited at the bottom of the driveway, which ran up a long stretch surrounded by thick pine and maple. Doc Campbell offered to put in some work on the farm if we could all stay for a while on some spare spot on the old guy's land. It wouldn't have gone so well if it weren't for the Reverend.

The farmer, I heard, had fought in the last big war. His oldest son hadn't believed in this one, would rather stay home and help tend the farm. His daddy was fine with his son never having to see or do the things he'd seen or done over there, but the draft came and got the son, and rather than dodge it somehow, he answered his country's call and went to war like his father before him. The father's heart was heavy over it, so the Reverend took him aside and counseled him. I still have no idea what the Reverend said to the old farmer, but by the end of that talk, the old man stood up and said we could all stay for a while on his land. Everyone was happy except Doc Campbell, who just got meaner and surlier.

We only knew a little more about Doc Campbell than we did about the Reverend. Like the farmer's son, he'd been against the war in Vietnam but he got drafted. Unlike most of us, he'd seen how it actually was over there. Then he took some combat injury to the head that left him half-blind and all-crazy, so he wound up dishonorably discharged. Some of the other guys in the group were also drafted soldiers who'd gone on the run while home on leave. Doc Campbell confided in them more than the rest of us. For all his hatred for the US government and the US military, he never stopped priding himself as a soldier, so he'd seen fit to appoint himself our leader. Hell, what were the rest of us supposed to do? *Someone* was taking charge of our shit show, keeping us organized and alert enough so we didn't starve or worse, and the rest of us were too high all the time to pull a mutiny or anything. It worked, for a while.

The Reverend had never challenged Doc Campbell's authority, nor did he volunteer himself for any kind of leadership, yet the more we listened to the Reverend, the more disenchantment set in about Doc Campbell.

Behind the farmhouse, there spread a great, rolling, green pasture. In the back, it dipped downhill and funneled into a short dark path through the woods, which led out into another field, this one steeper and rockier and thornier. It was no good for farming, but it suited our needs fine, so that's where we made camp, living off eighty acres of green and gold, for a month, maybe more. During the day, a lot of us worked on the farm. Sometimes the farmer's wife brought sandwiches and lemonade out to the workers, but the family never invited anyone inside. Downhill through the woods from our camp, there ran a wide, roaring creek. There were good spots there for taking baths and washing our clothes, other good spots for fishing.

On any night, there were always three or four campfires blazing, all spread out from each other amidst the cluster of tents and vehicles in the field, with different groups of our caravan family playing music, smoking grass and doing whatever other drugs were around when someone had them. We talked about the war, about the shit in Washington, whatever else was on anyone's mind. Whenever you roamed the campground, you might spot the Reverend just sitting around quietly listening wherever. Only when he caught you alone would he take over the conversation, in the wee hours when everyone else was passed out or winding down elsewhere, and you just happened to be the last guy or gal stirring by the dwindling embers. Then you'd look up and see him sitting across the coals from you, sometimes with his dog Providence panting at his side. He'd ask you what was on your mind, oh so unassuming. Before you knew it, you'd find yourself telling him your whole life story. At first, he'd just sit and listen.

Naturally, he'd ask about your religious upbringing, if any of it had stuck with you. If it hadn't, he wouldn't judge you, or if he did, he never said so. Instead he'd ask what sort of stories *had* stuck with you from your earlier years. Whatever your answer, he had a parable ready in response, just for you. No matter who you were, he had one that was just right.

Maybe you'd held onto some fond memories of your old Sunday-schooling in spite of yourself, something you hadn't thought of in years. He'd reach into his coat for his Bible and read you some story you'd never heard, of your favorite hero from the old or new testament. That voice of his alone was enough to cook it up into a fiery yarn, making it new again, so it burned itself into your mind's eye, full of sound and fury, signifying everything you'd never find your own words for, but would always carry afterwards, through some new light that belonged only to you. Or maybe it was a book of Greek or Norse mythology you recalled, from your old high school library before you turned on, tuned in, dropped out, and hit the road, or watching old Westerns on TV with your dad. You could bet he had a story to tell about that, too, from some new angle all the history books had left out, in his own words.

Some of us – mostly women – had taken ever so ethereally to some of those strange New Age witchy practices, calling it Wicca, the kind of stuff there are whole sections for in the book stores nowadays. The Reverend could tell you things about where all those new ideas really originated in ancient times, like the old Celtic days, before the Romans and the Normans tried to stamp it out, how what folks said about it today was a pale ghost of the old magic. When he spoke of it, you felt the *real* old magic, as though he'd been there himself, thousands of years ago, maybe as a High Priest, side by side with some High Priestess he still missed. He confided once, in the denouement of such a tale, that he found it unfair and mighty lonely, living in a day and age with only men out and about as preachers.

It never occurred to us that he might just be making it all up. It was real when he told it, and not just in our mind's eyes. Whenever he spoke like that, in the night around the dying campfire, the winds rose and howled through the surrounding forest, carrying in echoes from the times and places he spoke of. By the time he finished talking, you'd barely hear his words. Instead, you'd see and feel it, so whenever you went to sleep, the flames of the imagery roared on through your dreams. While you sat and listened, you'd swear it was all really going on, somewhere in the outer dark of the windswept forest. The trees sang with the blazing swords of angels and demons, of Odin and Loki or Zeus and Aphrodite, of the songs of Valkyries and Sirens, of thundering chariots, the clash of steel, the war-cries and booming Winchesters of Geronimo and Wyatt Earp, or the echoing chants of druids and witches around old standing stones.

Whenever you next woke, everyone you met would talk about the same sounds they'd heard all night, echoing through the surrounding woods. I knew something strange was going on, but I had no idea what. Then came my night around the dying fire with the Reverend.

I was sullen and awkward that night, and thankful for a chance to sit alone with the dwindling flames. I'd been fucking a girl who called herself Adelaide. So had my best friend Paul. Now she was pretty sure she was pregnant. She didn't know which of us was the father. All three of us were nervous and a little crazy, especially in this lifestyle we'd gotten used to. Both Adelaide and Paul were asleep with each other, while I sat up thinking just about everything a guy will think at a time like that. I looked up and saw the Reverend seated on a log across from me. His eyes studied me with melancholy compassion, in a way so I knew he knew.

"Where did you say you were from, Quincy?" he said.

"Florida," I said.

"Ah. I might have known the accent. I was on a picking crew in Florida for a time."

"That before you took up your ministry?"

"Oh, well after."

"My parents owned a vineyard," I said. "They put me to work on it as soon as I was old enough. Man, did they ever work my ass off! Oh, sorry..."

"Think nothing of it. So this taste of farming life is not new to you."

I shrugged. "I like it better all the way up here. Better company, for one thing, and it ain't always so damn...eh, sorry...ain't always so hot."

He drew up straighter and regarded me sternly. When the Reverend frowned at you, it was like his face turned into an angry question-mark. "You spend too much time correcting yourself in front of me, like you think I am too sensitive a soul, with virgin ears. Speak to me from your real mind, your real heart, your true soul, as you are. I will let you know if you offend me. If there are things in your mind you would rather not say to me, that is your business. Do not show me a face of false virtue, painted as you imagine I wish to see it. I have traveled more roads than you have dreamed of, boy. I have known angels and demons alike, and I have been both. I have no time for hypocrites."

Hearing that low, stern tone with those fierce eyes fixed on you, it felt like taking a bath in fire and brimstone. "Fuckin' A, man," I said. I was quiet for another moment. He waited. "Yeah. I like it better up in these parts."

"I thought I sensed a seasoned man of the land in you, or the makings of one." His voice was easy and friendly again. "Between you and I, these fine folk with whom we travel, I believe many of them took to it with more sheltered romantic notions than they have found in the reality of it...as seeds in the wind of the field."

I sighed. "Yeah, well, I could still say the same about some other things in my life."

"You will endure it, I think, as I pray so shall all in our caravan. I fear that most of them will not. That which does not kill you makes you stronger. It was a lost, mad, evil man who originally said that, but I believe he was correct on that point...or he ought to have been. We can all of us choose to be made stronger and wiser by that which we endure, or we may be left broken, cowardly and cruel by it. The latter is, to my mind, worse than death, worse than any flames of perdition that may await us on the other side, for it is a cold, clammy cave to be left crawling and groping blindly in." The Reverend gazed silently into the glowing embers, then leaned back and stretched his long arms with a loud groan. "These are good lands on which to toil, to make the body and soul strong. I have been in Vermont before. It is one of the finer states in this fine nation of ours."

"You know this area at all?"

"This town, Sturgeon, yes, I have been here before. To tell you the truth, though, boy, I do not recall much of it. I have heard tell of it, though."

The air changed subtly. The coals stirred between us. The trees beyond the field whispered a different tune.

"This is a fine land, a fine town, a fine area...but great evil has happened here. Many of the older folks whisper stories of it. Why, only the other day, I heard the farmer's wife talking to one of her friends. They are not the only ones I have listened to. They say that many years ago, evil men and women, desiring wealth and power they could not acquire by earthly nor honest means, conjured and struck foul deals with evil spirits...not the creatures of Satan, such as you may read about in this book I carry..." He took his Bible from his coat, held it up. "No, other preachers will tell that this book is the one word of truth. There is much truth herein, yes, but it is incomplete to the clouded mind...too easily distorted. No, there are beings from worlds far worse and stranger, from weirder, distant shores in the great beyond. They have interest in meddling with the dealings of Man, as surely as the devils and angels of Christ's paradise and Satan's perdition."

The last of the coals had gone out by now. The Reverend loomed across from me, an etching of solid black in the moonless night. The forest moaned, keeping rhythm with his speech, like the music in a movie, like the creatures he talked of had come to speak for themselves, through the whistling branches.

"This cabal of evil men and women," the Reverend wend on. "These foul beings with whom they trafficked called for a sacrifice in blood. They lured a young man into their fold, promising him a share in their power, and they took his life, feeding his soul to the devils of the Dark Lands. But there was something in this young man's soul they had not seen, some strength that lived on, something the fiends he'd been fed to could not hold. In his soul's defiance, he became a fiend himself, in his own right...something neither good nor evil, but vengeful, a thing made of scorched bone with razor-blade edges from head to toe. When next this cult performed their dark rituals, it was he that answered rather than the ones they had summoned. He harried them to their ruin. One by one, they were found throughout the countryside, torn asunder...but there was no blood on the ground where they were found, for the claws that rent their flesh were hot as perdition, cauterizing their wounds instantly.

"I don't know why I'm telling you all this, Quincy." He sighed and shook his head. "Perhaps it's because some of your blood is of these lands, and it called you to it, and that is why we are all here. Your kin might have turned us from their door, but these lands are still part of you as you are part of them, even though you did not grow up here. I do not believe that there is anything infernal in you, but I believe that – like the young man who became a fiend – there is strength within your soul beyond what you yourself can see. I hope in time you come to recognize and own it, and that it carries you through whatever is to come."

All I could find to say was, "Thanks, Reverend."

When I slept, I don't remember if I dreamed of the story the Reverend had told me. I'd already felt it all, as a waking dream, while I listened to his words. So had everyone else, while they slept or tried to sleep.

A few mornings later, I woke to the sound of Doc Campbell arguing with the Reverend. More and more lately, Doc Campbell found some excuse or other to antagonize the Reverend, calling him a snake-oil charlatan, filling everyone's head with all those old ideas that would make us slow and ruin us all. I don't think Doc Campbell ever sat and let the Reverend tell him a story. That last argument was particularly bad. It was the one time I ever heard and felt the real threat of physical violence in the Reverend's booming voice. I wondered how anyone could be as crazy or stupid as Doc Campbell, to keep snarling at him at that point. Finally they stormed away from each other, so I went back to sleep.

A day or so later, we realized the Reverend was gone. Providence kept coming up to everyone, yipping and jumping, making a fussier nuisance of himself than usual. Before much longer, the old farmer came hobbling down through the field. Our nighttime revels – our music and our campfires and howls of laughter and all – were scaring his livestock and keeping his family awake. Doc Campbell tried to reason with him. Finally the farmer stormed off, back up the hill.

Doc Campbell kept assuring us that he'd talk sense into the old bastard, one way or another. You might think one of those AWOL soldiers with us would have stood up to Doc Campbell now, but they just weren't fighters at heart, no matter what had happened to them or what they'd been forced to do over there. That's why they were here with us instead. They'd seen guys like Doc Campbell over there, though. What they saw coming out in him now scared them. It scared us all.

This time when Doc Campbell started shouting and barking orders, Providence started growling at him. That's when the sky darkened, letting out its own growls and snaps and barks in the distance. Doc Campbell shouted for someone to shut the damn dog up. When none of us did, he stormed over to the big spray-painted bus, went in, and came back out with his old service pistol. He shot Providence dead in front of everyone.

It was starting to sprinkle rain by the time the old farmer stormed back down into the field. Okay, he said, he'd put up with a bunch of drugged-out, dirty hippies camping out on his land, but now we were shooting guns off like lunatics. We didn't even have a man of God keeping us in line anymore. When he noticed the dead dog lying in the dampening dirt, he left and came back brandishing a shotgun, told us to pack up and leave right now.

Doc Campbell walked right up to the farmer, put the pistol against his cheek, and blew his face out the back of his head. By then, the sky was falling pretty hard. Doc Campbell waved his smoking pistol around and shouted that there were more bullets for anyone else who wanted to take an attitude with him. Then he stomped off uphill through the pouring rain, lost from sight in the gale before he even reached the short path through the trees. Before long, three more shots boomed out in the distance.

Some of us hoped there'd been another gun up at the house, and that the farmer's wife had used it on Doc Campbell when he came for her and the kids. But the sound of Doc Campbell's gun was fresh in our minds, its cordite stink still in our noses. The smart thing to do would be to pile into the vehicles and take off right then. Doc Campbell had the key to the bus, though. There wasn't enough room in the other vehicles for everyone. Besides, the storm was too torrential by now to drive out of the steep field.

Everyone ran for whatever shelter we had, dreading whatever would happen when Doc Campbell returned. Whoever we had to be close with, we clutched them to us tight. In the back of the van, Adelaide and Paul and I all held each other in a circle, forgave each other all the drama over Adelaide getting pregnant, and said we loved each other. I thought of the story the Reverend had told me, of the strength he claimed to see in me. I prayed he was right, prayed he hadn't just been jerking my chain to make me feel better, about my sorry little situation that seemed so inconsequential now. Either way, I hugged Adelaide and Paul as close as I could, told myself I'd call on the strength of these lands in my blood as the Reverend had put it, and protect both of them, however I had to, if it came to it. Sometimes the only thing that gets you through the night is telling yourself it's all about you.

The rising deluge outside made roaring brooks that gushed downhill, turning the field to mud. Clumps of tall grass slid out of the once-firm earth by the roots. Peering through the window, I saw the bodies of Providence and the farmer slip and slide against each other, downhill through the mud. They settled in a clump against one of the front wheels of another vehicle. They looked like they'd decided to hang out there together, flopping limply in the pounding deluge. The water pulled the farmer free and he disappeared downhill towards the woods, while Providence stayed put. The more the ground turned to sludge, the more the bus around us tilted and slid. We wondered if any of us would still be there by the end.

The storm turned the sky so dark, we couldn't tell when the day turned to dusk. It raged on like that all night. Within it, other things howled and clanged, out in the wind-battered trees around the field...all sorts of noises that didn't belong there in backwater Vermont. Morning found us all still there in the slanting field.

One by one, in a daze, we stumbled out into a bright new day. The whole world stank of soggy rot, marinating around us in the morning sun. The bodies of Providence and the farmer were gone. We never found either of them. We found Doc Campbell, a short distance uphill. He hung dangling upright in a tall pine, a piece of debris that had been swept up in the wind and caught there to flutter like a Christmas-tree ornament. His clothes were torn to shreds, showing deep slashes and lacerations all over his skin. Even down here, I could see that none of them bled, like all the blood had washed out of him in the rain.

Finally, I volunteered to climb up there and shove Doc Campbell out of the tree. When I made it up through all the scratchy branches, I found that both his hands had been impaled on two sharp ends, like someone had crucified him. I braced myself against the trunk and kicked at him 'til he came loose, sailed down, and landed with a thump on the mud and grass below.

By the time I made it down, the others had gathered around the body. He didn't smell so pretty, but like I said, neither did anything else. He was in a stranger state than we'd first thought. His open wounds were so clean, not because the rain had washed him out, but because they'd been instantly cauterized by whatever had gotten hold of him...like he'd been torn apart by white-hot vengeful claws.

It turned out that Adelaide had had a miscarriage during the storm. Paul died of an overdose two years later. I occasionally still talk to Adelaide over the Internet. She eventually got married and had some kids that lived. She lives out in Kansas now, runs a spirituality shop, and volunteers at a battered women's shelter. Last I checked, she and her husband were in the middle of a messy divorce. I teach self-defense courses at the local gym, have been engaged twice, but never made it to the altar. I still don't have any kids that I know of. Reading Adelaide vent about her marital woes makes me feel like less of an old loser about it.

I never saw the Reverend again, and to my knowledge, neither did anyone else. Something tells me I'm not gonna get a friend request from him on Facebook.

The Proper Word is Blackmail

One

The dining room looked and smelled like a freshly opened mausoleum. Even the elaborate furnishings stank of rot. At least the white cloth that draped the long table seemed fresh. Oil lamps lit the room, the glass caked in sticky grime, speckled in dead bugs, so the lamplight cast a grainy sheen over everything. Thick green curtains shut out the stars and moonlight.

Near the center of the table sat two men clad all in black, one in his later fifties, the other in his mid-twenties. Two more chaps stood behind them, dressed in neatly pressed servant's clothes. Large white napkins draped their folded hands, politely concealing the revolvers they held. Across from them, the host paced back and forth. He peered at the two guests with narrow, twitchy eyes. Through the kitchen doorway behind him, a stove roared and crackled, flushing the musty air with the scent of ash and meat. Violins sang through a scratchy phonograph. T'was a tranquil enough old tune, 'til some stray gust of air pushed the kitchen door wider, so it filled the air with the dizzy dissonance of the warped wax cylinder. A sixth man emerged, wearing a grease-stained chef's jacket and billowy white chef's hat. He set an ovular porcelain platter in front of each guest. Neither was given tableware.

The older man's grizzled, granite face twisted against the aroma of fresh biscuits and juicy, bleeding roast. "Do you expect us to eat with our bare hands, then?"

"I thought it wise," said the host, "at least until we've all had a civilized chat." His clothes had once been a gentleman's dinner finery. The suit had gone unwashed and untailored for so long that the trousers could likely stand up on their own. Grotesque discoloration splotched the edges of his gaunt, sunken-eyed face. In the curious light, the bulging veins in his forehead and long neck looked dark green. He peered at the younger man. "It wouldn't do, for either of you to mistake a fork or carving knife for a weapon."

"Look here," said the older guest, "if you think we're about to debase ourselves like monkeys in a –" Ripping, slurping, munching sounds rose from his left. He glanced over wearily. "Hawthorne, seriously?"

"Well, you know, Inspector…Mmmmm…You oughtn't let yours go cold. We must keep up our strength." The younger guest chewed and swallowed. He was slender, clean-shaven, pale as bleached bone with short-clipped black hair, blazing green eyes and a deep, livid scar that streaked one cheek temple to jawline. He lifted the roast with his bare hands and tore into it whole. He pulled a biscuit in half and soaked up bloody juice from his plate, smiling at their host. "Mister Swan here has himself a fine cook." His voice rose a notch and he shot glances at the surrounding figures. "Be grateful for a spot of wine, though, so I would."

"Assuming it's not poisoned." Inspector Francis Hawkins of Scotland Yard glared at their jittery, pacing host.

"Honestly, Inspector." Frederick Hawthorne leaned back in his chair and stretched both long arms. "There's at least half of a mile of thick forest, between us and any civilization, in a house given up for deserted or haunted, with pistols at our heads. You really think they'd waste good poison on us?"

Their coats hung on a rack behind them to the left, next to the door through which they'd entered. The contents of their pockets lay on a smaller table next to their host, arranged neatly like a scientific exhibit. The host hadn't bothered keeping track of which items belonged to whom. There were two timepieces, a length of cord, some coins and notes, a set of handcuffs, a loaded revolver, spare cartridges, the badge of a Scotland Yard Inspector, a small, worn-edged photograph of a pretty girl, and a sizable pocketknife with the razor-edged blade partially unfolded.

The host leaned towards them across the table. His voice dropped to an icy whisper. "You'd best heed your young friend's advice, Inspector Hawkins. You fellows have a lot to tell me, so make yourselves comfortable."

"Think the word won't get out that you've abducted a policeman?" The Inspector's face twisted ferally. "And here I'd heard you knew something about the eyes and ears of Whitechapel."

"Aye, that I do. They showed me straight to you and your clandestine meddling, didn't they now? As for your friends at the Yard, I'm sure they'd be keen on what those eyes and ears have told me about you...you and your favorite little Whitechapel informant."

Frederick Hawthorne drew upright. "Whitecha – *He's my bloody Scotland Yard informant!*"

Hawkins rolled his eyes and said through his teeth, "*Hawthorne, shut up.*"

"No use in subterfuge, Inspector." Mister Swan's voice kept vacillating curiously between a stilted high-society affectation and his own coarse East End roots. "Mister Hawthorne and I, we go well back…Yes, Mister Hawthorne?"

Frederick Hawthorne shrugged and ate more. His plate was already half cleared.

Swan went on, "You thought none of those eyes and ears were still mine. Inspector, I advise you, the sooner your young informant reunites me with a bit of stolen property, the sooner we can discuss your possible futures."

Frederick Hawthorne looked about. "Who – Now what in the –"

"*The carving, of the King of the Gods of Leonid,*" the host spat.

"Mate, you mean to tell me, you're *still* hung up over that ol' sham?"

A great fist crashed on the table next to Frederick's left hand. It came from over his shoulder. A cold ring of metal jammed against the back of his neck. "That's quite enough –"

The host barked over Frederick's head, "Did I tell you to do anything?"

The gun withdrew from Frederick's neck. "Sorry, Mister Swan." The fist stayed next to Frederick on the table, too close. "But really, I'd like to hear that sharp mouth of his after I –"

"Later. I've not decided to what extent." Swan's eyes met Frederick's. "If you've no care for yourself, Mister Hawthorne, I suggest you think of your old policeman friend here."

Frederick let his breath out slowly through his nose. He slid his elbows a little wider, so his shoulders relaxed. He glanced again at the gorilla-sized arm and fist next to him. He suspected the gun hadn't gone far from his head. He still smelled the oil on the metal. "What makes you think I give a toss about a bloody meddlesome copper?"

Swan nodded to the bloke behind Inspector Hawkins. The big man snatched a handful of the Inspector's silver hair, slammed him forward across the table like a pimp about to break in a fresh young harlot, and jammed the gun behind his ear. Before he could help himself, Frederick rose partway, shifting sidewise. The man behind him shoved him back in his chair, and jabbed him with the gun barrel again. The hand on his shoulder felt like thick old leather wrapped in steel bone, with an iron beam of an arm behind it. Hawkins's eyes blazed in Frederick's peripheral vision.

"Done pretending I don't know some things about you, Mister Hawthorne?" Swan asked.

"Fine, fine, there you have me." Frederick's voice stayed steady and hard. "Care to let the bloody meddlesome copper get comfy again?"

Mister Swan rolled his eyes and nodded. The man holding Hawkins let go and drew back, with more sharp cruelty than with which he'd attacked. Hawkins inhaled fiercely. He seemed to inflate upright like a hitherto withered balloon.

"What's it you want to know, mate?" Frederick tore off another bite of roast. The gun eased away from his head. The iron hand on his shoulder relaxed slightly.

"The carving. It's in either your possession or Robert Powell's. If you could point me towards his whereabouts —"

"I don't wager either's gone far," said Frederick, "from where I last left 'em."

"Oh? Where's that?"

"Partway up New Gravel Lane from the docks, there's a set of stairs, leading down to a canal. There you'll find a lonely doorway, leading into an old locked deserted store space." Frederick took another bite. His plate was nearly clean. He cast his eyes about at the gunmen. "I trust you lads know the spot I mean, aye?"

"Don't talk to them," Swan spat. "They'll speak when I tell 'em to."

"Aye, anyhow, there's a storm drain with a rusty loose cover, pulls right —"

Swan's hands and lips shook worse and worse. "I know the damned spot! Powell's not hiding there. We've looked. Stop lying!"

"I ain't lying." Frederick sighed at his nearly empty plate. "Aye, of course you've already looked there, and I tell you, what you want is still right under your nose."

"Show me to it, then. I'll judge for myself."

"Gladly, though there's the problem. See, I smashed the carving to smithereens whilst Powell crawled groveling for it at my feet, right down there by the water. Funny about ol' Powell, he was already bleeding out, but soon as I smashed that space-rock to pieces, he withered right away, to a dusty skeleton. So for whatever it's worth, you was right and I was wrong. There *was* something to all that mumbo-jumbo, over which you and your mates was murdering each other along with half of London."

Swan's face gleamed with sweat. He loomed in and smacked both hands across the tabletop. "You can't have destroyed it! That's not possible! I must find my way back, to… to…"

Swan blazed with so much desperate violence that even his underlings recoiled. Frederick drew back in his chair as if recoiling with them. In the same motion, he lifted his plate and turned it sideways. The last bloody little gob of roast slid off and hit the table with a splat. Frederick brought the plate down on the table's edge, so it shattered into three jagged porcelain shards. He rose and spun, face to face with the shocked bloke still lifting the pistol. The shard of plate sank deep into the base of the gunman's neck, so swift and deep that Frederick barely felt it, shattered porcelain being deadlier sharp than any razor-edged metal. Blood went everywhere, including all over Frederick. His free hand closed on the man's gun wrist.

The other gunman's pistol rose, so the barrel left Hawkins's head. The grouchy old bastard seemed to catch the idea, lucky enough. Hawkins sprang up, spun, and drove all his weight through his shoulder against his enemy's back. The arm flew wild. A shot shook the room. A tube of air puffed and fluttered across Frederick's shirt. His chest froze for an instant. Wood split in the ceiling somewhere, and most of his mind registered that the bullet had missed him. Now he had his own guard's gun in hand. He squeezed the trigger. Behind Hawkins, the other gunman hopped, spun and dropped with a crash. Frederick's man clutched at the shard of porcelain in his neck, even while he kept trying to grapple with Frederick. Frederick sent him off with a kick. The big blighter's weight carried him careening away. He struck the nearest wall headfirst, flopped to the floor, and stayed there floundering.

Across the table, Davy Swan turned and scrambled for the pile of his captives' possessions. In that pile, there lay Hawkins's service revolver. The Inspector sprang and hoisted himself atop the table, with all the considerable vitality he'd kept through the waning years from his soldier days in India. He dashed and leapt, tackling Swan to the floor, just as the latter's hand closed on the revolver. Frederick circled the table as the other two wrestled for the gun. Someone squeezed off a stray shot. It punched through the wall next to Frederick's foot, so he ducked backwards.

The gun was in Swan's hand, but that hand was already squeezed and twisted in Hawkins's surer grasp. Hawkins pistoned his free elbow across Swan's jaw and smacked the gun hand against the floor a few times. Finally, the fingers slackened and the pistol slid free. Hawkins dragged Swan away across the stiff, grimy carpet, one elbow around Swan's neck, the other hand fumbling blindly for the small table where lay his and Frederick's affects. Finally he found the handcuffs. He wrestled himself to his feet, dragged his opponent onto his knees and cuffed him from behind.

Hawkins panted and heaved, not as young as he'd once been after all. He braced his feet wide and held Swan low. Frederick strode to Hawkins's side and loomed over Swan. His breath went in and out through his teeth, in low snarls. He cast one venomous glare at Swan before he retrieved his pocketknife from the pile.

A wild shriek split the calm. From the kitchen doorway, there sprang the cook who'd earlier delivered the food. He barreled forward, eyes wild, still wearing his puffy white cloud of a hat, brandishing a cleaver high. Frederick hunched in surprise, then snapped up and about. He thumbed open his blade and lifted it so the attacker's swinging arm skewered itself. The hand spasmed open so the cleaver fell. Frederick caught the cleaver, slung it about, and drove it with all his might into the cook's skull. The juicy crunch quivered through his bones and muscles, all the way to his shoulder. The man landed with a thud at Frederick's feet and sprawled quivering.

In the sickly, spectral light, Frederick's blazing green eyes looked less human than ever. He circled the table slowly, in a smoldering trance. The man with a bullet in his chest groaned and crawled towards the other fellow's dropped pistol. He clawed for it, nearly there. Frederick placed a foot on the blighter's back, yanked his head up by the hair and pressed the blade's edge beneath one corner of the jaw. He stooped to meet the bleary, hateful eyes, stared deep into them, then jerked sidewise and slit the throat ear to ear. He stepped over the spasming, spurting body. His soles gingerly evaded the spreading dark puddle. Once more, he circled the table to Inspector Hawkins's side.

By now, the policeman faced his prostrate captive. "Looking quite green at the gills, this one," Hawkins managed. Labored breathing felled his intended bravado.

"Aye, quite literally, perhaps," Frederick growled, "but that's another matter. So here you are, like you wanted, some poor bugger to prop up before a judge."

"I welcome the hangman," Swan rasped, "for the Gods of the Stars await me yet. Oh yes, I'll confess all to the court, proudly. I'll be sure to tell them all about what gallant heroes it was, what brought me to justice…this here *respected officer of the law*, in cahoots with a lowly

Whitechapel murderer. Oh, won't they love to finally hear it!"

Hawkins scowled. "Indeed. So who you do you think they'll likelier believe, me with solid evidence of at least a dozen murders you've committed or been party to, or you with your blasted star-cult conspiracy?"

"Oh, I could name dozens more witnesses, what could tell them all about your crimes, with this green-eyed wolf you've covered up for. Oh, they'd call me a liar, no doubt. They'd still look into what I'd told 'em, wouldn't they, even after I've hanged? They'll have to. You both know it, sure as I. How long you expect this game of yours to last? Sooner or later, it'll come down to it between you, won't it, so it's one or the –"

A fresh flash and crack lit the din. Davie Swan's brains spat from the back of his skull. The rest of him pitched backwards, as though leaping to catch up with them. Hawkins stood frozen, staring at the smoking barrel at the end of his outstretched arm.

Frederick scowled at the corpse at their feet. He hissed at Inspector Hawkins, "If this means you have to drag me all over London again, to sniff out another hangman's prize, I'll be quite cross."

Hawkins's arm dropped to his side, as though the pistol he held had turned to a block of lead. For a moment, he eyed Frederick with defeated disgust, as though it was Frederick who'd squeezed the trigger. "No. No, I'll file it all as…something else. You needn't concern yourself further, Hawthorne." He shuddered and peered at Frederick. "Oh, what, all of a sudden, you don't approve?"

Frederick shrugged, turned, went and retrieved their coats from the rack in the corner. "Oh, lil' ol' me? No objections here, no." He put his own coat back on, then draped the other over the older man's shoulders. After that, he reclaimed his timepiece, the garroting cord, Clara's photograph, and half the pile of money. He pocketed all of that, then turned back and pressed something into the Inspector's palm. "I ain't the one this belongs to, is all."

Hawkins opened his hand and looked down at his own badge.

Two

Frederick took an oil lamp from the wall, wiped some bug-crusted grime from the glass, and headed for the parlor.

Hawkins followed the bobbing glow through the dark, deserted house. "Fancy all that mad rubbish he was spouting, eh? *Gods waiting for him in the stars.* And you, stringing him out with it like that – *Some ancient scoundrel with his youth preserved by the funny little space rock...*I say, you ought to write for the penny dreadfuls –"

The blood on Frederick's shirt and face stood out bright and wet in the lamp's glare. His green eyes caught the light and glowed like a cat's. He wore a peculiar little smile.

Hawkins paused, cleared his throat, then went on, "Well, in any case, there's the last of it, yes? So let's find our way out of here, back to the city, before –"

"Oh, not so fast." Frederick mounted the staircase. "You're a policeman after all, a right honorable servant of the crown."

"Yes, but we agreed –"

"Aye, so here we are at a fresh crime scene. You wouldn't think of popping off before having a look at all the evidence, would you now?" Frederick paused midway up and looked back. "You really think for a second I'd let you pull me into this, if there weren't something in it for me? As the late unlamented Mister Swan mentioned…" He made the rest of his way upstairs, into a dark hallway.

"Don't play the brigand with me," said Hawkins, following along. "If I didn't think better of you, I'd have seen you to the gallows long ago –"

"When I say *me*, I of course mean the good folks of Whitechapel, what frequent my humble establishment. Swan and them louts have hidden out here for months. I'd have liked to leave 'em here to rot."

"Then why didn't you?"

Frederick motioned for silence. As he moved through the narrow gloom, the lantern lowered at his side, all but forgotten, as another set of senses altogether overtook him. Whenever he passed a doorway, he slowed, his ears twitched, and his nostrils flared. Finally, he stopped at a door and tried a knob. He found it locked, stepped back and drove his foot hard against it. The bolt splintered and the door swung inward, revealing a black void broken only by two curtained windows that floated side by side.

A tiny gasp echoed in the stillness. It was hard to tell where it came from. Something shifted and scuttled. Hawkins lifted his pistol and pressed his back against the wall beside the door. Frederick motioned for him to lower it then stepped into the room, the lamp extended. Hawkins followed. The light fell across the shape of a woman, or what was left of her, still somewhat alive. What torn garments she'd been allowed to keep didn't hide the ruined, caked, crusted state of her thighs and mouth.

Frederick fought down his gorge, wished he hadn't eaten so recently, and knelt next to her. "There, there, it's all right... We ain't with –"

He'd known better than to touch her in the slightest, but his knuckles accidentally brushed her knee. She shrieked. He hopped upright and drew back, nerves quivering.

Hawkins approached, put a hand on Frederick's shoulder and urged him further away. He then knelt by the girl, keeping a better distance. "Look here, you needn't be afraid. I'm a policeman. My friend there, he helped me find you, helped me stop those dreadful men who were harming you. He...was hurt by them. But they shan't hurt anyone anymore."

After a moment, she seemed to understand. She still looked ready to shriek the roof off the house. She stared with fresh alarm, past Hawkins. He looked back. Frederick had peeled off his ruined shirt and was fishing through the closet.

"Who is she?" asked Hawkins.

"Why, the lady of the house." Frederick approached again and waved the lamp so her plain gold ring glistened. "Mrs. Dolores Ellington." The woman twitched, perhaps at the sound of her own name.

"Then...her husband...the rest of the family...you suppose...?"

"No." Frederick spat on the floor. "Swan had some dirt on her husband, so the man kept away from his own house."

"Who –"

"Richard Ellington. You'll find him in a townhouse near Buckingham Court, Number Twenty-Three."

"Not Richard Ellington, of Ellington Carriage Manufacturers…"

"Aye, that one. I'll wager it was a coach from his own factory what carried us here blindfolded. The ol' baron's put a great deal of effort into looking like the respectable family man, which includes keeping his proclivities towards the Chinaboys in Limehouse secret. He thought Swan was just another business partner, until Swan fell into some trouble, and needed a place to hide out. So he went to his ol' chum Ellington, and decided to find out just how much the swine was willing to offer up, to keep his proclivities secret. We've seen how the place has fared without a housekeeper."

"How did you piece all that together?"

"As to Ellington's double-life? Oh, there's no secrets in The Devil's Draft, Inspector, not if you knows what gossip to listen to from the customers and how to put it together. As to Swan's hideout, you told me the last of what I needed to know just the other night, as you drank off-duty in my place. Figured you'd come 'round asking for my help, looking for Swan…"

"I'll have you know, my superiors wanted me to incriminate you with him –"

"Nice to know the Yard ain't forgotten about me. It's all turned out splendidly."

Hawkins sighed and shrugged. "So there's extortion added to Mister Swan's crimes."

"The proper word is blackmail," said Frederick. "Or is the laws really written oh so different, for crimes done onto them posh pillars of society?"

"Spare me your anarchist ravings for one night, and help me get this poor girl –"

"*Poor girl, poor girl...*" The murmur came from Dolores Ellington. Both men's eyes shot to her. Her head lolled, and she stared off at nothing in particular. "That's what the poor cook said whenever he saw me, when the others brought me out to use me. They wouldn't let the cook use me, so he'd shake his head, go about his duties, and mutter *poor girl, poor girl.* I said once, *Poor cook, poor cook,* but the others slapped me and hurt me worse and told me to keep quiet. *Poor cook...*He never used me...He didn't see...None of them saw it, none of them felt it, coming out of their noses, out of their mouths, out of their ears...He didn't like what the masters who brought him along did...I...I don't like what they'll do to you..."

"Oh, don't worry no more about them, lass," said Hawkins. "I told you, they're beyond harming you or –"

Frederick clamped a hand on Hawkins's shoulder. "Quiet, you old jingo." He leaned in on the girl. "What was that, about something coming out of their ears and mouths and noses?"

"The...the golden-green mist...It was golden-green, and it...it...You've killed them all now, yes?"

"Aye, love," said Frederick. "They's all done in. How many bloody times we needs –?"

"Hawthorne, for pity's sake," barked Hawkins, "stop tormenting the –"

"Aye, I know, the *poor girl, poor girl.* I heard her when she said it. Now she's on to bigger, better things." Frederick's glowing green eyes met Mrs. Ellington's. "Go on, love, you're doing splendidly."

"The golden-green mist...It wanted out...They need

only have died…They would have before long either way, you know. Now so will I. Now so will you."

Before Frederick could press the point, something echoed from downstairs. Hawkins spun back towards the door and cocked his pistol.

"It will do you no good," muttered Mrs. Ellington. *"Poor brutes, poor brutes…"*

Hawkins's fingers shook as he snapped open the cylinder. He steadied his hand as he dropped in fresh cartridges, chamber upon chamber. Footsteps shambled in the landing below, then started up the stairs.

"Hawkins," hissed Frederick, "did you bother to keep either of the pistols them louts was holding at our heads?"

"I…I…"

"You didn't, did you?"

"No. But what in the blazes…We had a good look at the rest of the house. No one else was downstairs. The door was bolted. How could anyone else have gotten in without —"

"Whatever you do, don't poke an inch of your head out the door. Just twist your hand out and fire a few shots out into that hall, at the stairwell."

"But —"

"Just do it."

Hawkins rose, crept across the carpet, and stuck his hand out through the doorway. He snapped off two shots. Four more came back, lighting up the dim hallway like lightning flashes. Only three of the shots slammed into the upstairs walls outside. Hawkins flattened his back against the inner wall next to the doorway, chest heaving. The footsteps continued upward, faster, shambling worse.

Mrs. Ellington opened her mouth to scream. Frederick

sprang, grabbed her in both arms, and clamped a hand over her mouth. She tried to thrash, but he held her utterly still as though in an iron vice. Her eyes bulged with reawakened terror, no doubt certain she was back in the clutches of her late tormenters. Frederick hated himself for putting her through more such terror, but he dragged her from where she'd huddled, into one of the corners of the room to the right of the door, across from Hawkins. The shambling feet drew nearer. Strange sounds echoed through the hallway, from the throats of the unseen foes, which sounded less and less human the nearer they drew.

Frederick hissed at Hawkins, "Back off into your opposite corner. Aye, that way. Just fire off the rest of your shots at whatever comes through that door."

Hawkins obeyed. Frederick edged towards the doorway, his back against the wall. He kept Mrs. Ellington pressed and muffled against him. When they were halfway there, his arms snapped open, freeing her. It was like loosing a bowstring with an arrow that shrieked. With an ear-splitting banshee-cry, she ran into the middle of the room, just as the invaders entered. In the lead came David Swan. His head still leaked on both sides from Hawkins's bullet. His neck also leaked from one of his companion's shots, the one that hadn't punched the hallway wall. All three lurching bodies swelled and roiled, their mouths and ears and noses puffing out glowing golden-green dust. It even leaked in rivulets from their trousers, as though coming out of their arses and cock-slits too. Whatever was inside them generating it, it puffed their midsections ever fatter, closer to bursting through their shirts.

At first, it seemed Hawkins would lose his nerve and freeze up staring. Then he lifted his revolver and emptied it into the men. They spun and fired back wildly, in the general directions of both Hawkins and Mrs. Ellington, for as long as their human hands remained in one piece. The bodies split like ruptured grapes, so their guns clattered to the floor. Up from the falling husks, beings spewed into the air with frothing jaws and empty eyes of ancient, elemental hatred, their bodies formed entirely from the swirling spectral dust.

Thanks to the two distractions, the remains of the human shells hadn't yet noticed Frederick. The wrathful angels within them smelled just who to look for, though, right away. They swelled to fill the room. Frederick strode calmly to meet them. They drooled and grinned down at the foolhardy mortal who dared to bait them forth. He held still as they closed in around him. As their jaws opened to crush him and rip him apart between them, he lifted and opened his pocketknife. The blade he wielded glowed with the same otherworldly light as themselves, and not just for how the metal caught their light.

The swirling monsters paused in a moment's confusion. It was all the time Frederick needed. In that instant, he darted left and right, as though closing with two mortal foes. He made two neat, clean slices across their necks. The wounds split wide. As they recoiled, the room went dark.

Finally, Frederick found another lamp and managed to light it. By now, the glowing, living dust had drifted off, back into whatever other realm of energetic vibrational existence, along with the corpses of the angels they'd formed. The mortal coils within which they'd gestated lay strewn about like ruptured seed-pods, except still made of human meat and bone, so they'd splattered all over the walls, not to mention all over Inspector Hawkins and Mrs. Ellington. Hawkins still pressed his back into the corner, his pistol on the floor next to him. Mrs. Ellington had retreated to the same spot where they'd first found her, curled up tighter than ever into a shivering little ball.

Frederick looked them over. No bullets had struck them. Finally he managed to rouse Hawkins back to some sort of lucid, coherent state.

Hawkins wiped dripping gore from his face. "What…the…bloody hell…just happened?"

"More or less what I expected," said Frederick. "Seems Swan and his mates absorbed more of what their star-cult had to offer than they realized. For now, let's just find our way out of here. You could no doubt use a bath before reporting in to Scotland Yard."

As they saw the lady out to the carriage, she kept looking at both of them and mumbling, "*Poor brutes…poor brutes…*"

Three

Three days later, The Devil's Draft pub opened in the late afternoon on Whitechapel Road. Among the evening's first customers was a finely dressed gentleman, pale and slouched and caked in sweat, looking like he'd not slept in weeks. From behind the bar, Frederick met his eyes halfway between the door and a bar stool, in a way that made the fellow hunch up and approach slower.

The man reached the bar, removed his hat and held it against his chest. "Mister…Mister Frederick Hawthorne?"

Frederick arched one eyebrow and scowled slightly.

"My name is Mister Richard Ellington. I...I...you'll have heard of me."

"Of Ellington Carriage Manufacturers. Aye."

"I've just come from the hospital, where...where my wife convalesces. The doctors say she's likely to pull through." A hint of a smile touched the timid lips. "I received the news personally, two days ago, from Inspector Francis Hawkins of Scotland Yard. He mentioned your name, and your establishment here."

"Did he now?"

"Sir, you are...a truly great citizen, a wonderful man. I thought it only right that I come thank you personally."

"That what you already just now done?" Frederick said hopefully.

"I...Yes, sir. Thank you."

"Aye, seems fortune's favored you both ways, which I understand is how you prefers it – a fact that's still a secret to your lofty circle. Now you have your wife *and* your house back, with your reputation intact, without a drop of your own blood spilt."

Mister Ellington trembled worse. "Indeed, though...not a secret to everyone, it seems."

"There's no such thing as a secret here in The Devil's Draft. Anyhow, your buggery's nothing to me. If your wife recovers and chooses to stay with you, after what you fed her to, well...Look here, if you brought money, sit down, shut up, and have a drink. Otherwise, get out."

Mister Ellington hunched up like a kicked dog, turned, and trudged towards the door.

Frederick looked up sharply. "Just a minute."

Mister Ellington froze and shrank up in the doorway.

He turned back slowly. As he approached the bar again, Frederick drew a slip of paper and started scrawling something on it. "Here's some fine chaps I know, what often drink here after toiling the day away in your factory. I'm sure they'd each appreciate a higher salary…which of course shan't be docked should I ever need to borrow their services on your time." Frederick handed the list over. "Oh, and also your coachman. He needs a raise as well. He still keeps the hours he held as of…" Frederick drew a ledger from beneath the bar and consulted it. "…the fifteenth of last month, yes?"

"Well, yes, but…" Mister Ellington looked back and forth from the list to Frederick. "I say, this is preposterous!"

"As I said, there's no secrets in The Devil's Draft." Frederick's face split into a sly, icy grin. "Care to keep your secrets in here, do you?"

"But…but what use could one of your class possibly have for –"

"That's my business."

"Very well." Mr. Ellington gulped deeply. "It would seem I've traded one extortionist for another."

"The proper word," said Frederick Hawthorne, "is blackmail."

Nagga Mountain Blues

The sun hadn't set. This year's summer festival was still warming up. Drummers thrummed out rhythms for the orgy of dancers that thickened and thrashed around the raging bonfire. Towering trees swayed around the clearing through the soft, warm wind, moving with the dancers. I sat on the railing of the elevated porch of the village's long, ancient gathering hall, a half-empty jug of sap-wine dangling from my fist, thinking I might join the dancers soon, watching for any of the village girls I liked. My body felt strained through and through from working the field all day, but I felt my second wind coming on, any minute now.

Shelov, my brother, leaned against the railing, his thick arms crossed over his chest, his long, silky hair tied back from his hard, scarred face. Sometimes I offered him a swig of sap-wine. Occasionally he yanked it from me, swigged and passed it back. Other times, he half-glanced at me and waved it away. I reminded myself not to get too shitfaced, too fast. At midnight, I meant to gather with the other young braves for the Howling Hunt. They'd asked Shelov to lead the ritual, to which he just said, "Fuck the Howling Hunt." So far, he wasn't much for conversation tonight. His eyes smoldered, like they did a lot since he came home.

Through the light throng, a Spirelight girl hurried uphill, clad in nothing but a light hemp slip. Shelov's eyes fixed on her. I shrugged. Shelov liked Spirelight girls. I didn't. He was younger than me, but had traveled more, seen more of Deschemb, had tasted the wines and women of many lands. Me, I was still getting used to Spirelights living among us up in these hills. All social prejudices aside, I just wasn't into solid-shaded light-meat.

The Spirelight girl got closer. She was crying. Her slip was ripped, and she held one side of the top up to her shoulder. She couldn't be older than fourteen, petite with gleaming, baby-smooth skin. Anyone who tried to get close and talk to her, she evaded them, shuddered, and quickened her pace. She made for the far side of the gathering hall, as if to slip around back. Shelov jackknifed himself over the fifteen-foot railing, landed on his feet without crouching, and stalked towards her. When she tried to shrug him off, he caught her by the shoulders and looked her dead in the eyes. She squirmed futilely, staring, more terrified of him than whatever she'd been running from.

Great, I thought, *there's still light in the sky, and he's already a problem.* I hopped up, took the stairs off the porch, circled and trotted towards them.

"What's goin' on, girl?" said Shelov. "Come on, speak up. It's okay, baby girl, I got you. I ain't gonna hurt you."

She didn't look like she believed him. Given how Shelov came across at the best of times, I didn't blame her.

I put a hand on his shoulder, was glad he didn't elbow me in the face, stepped up next to him, and said, "It's okay, miss. We're the good guys. You can trust us. What's wrong?"

I had a kinder face than Shelov, so she settled down a little. "Can I just...Uh...You boys don't mind the company of a Spirelight girl? Out in the open, where it's safe, I mean?"

Shelov and I looked at each other, looked back to her, shrugged, and said in unison, "Not at all."

We walked her back up to the porch of the gathering hall. Some folks wandered in and out, not paying us much mind. Fortunately, my sap-wine jug still sat where I'd left it on the railing. I offered her a swig. She accepted it graciously and took a deep chug. When she handed it back, I confess I frowned at how much less it weighed. She sniffed and wiped her nose. Tears flowed freer down her cheeks. She'd forgotten to hold onto the torn strap, so the cloth had fallen, showing off a lot more of her. Rising red marks covered her pale flesh. I was used to women bred of these hills, a tougher sort than these Spirelights who were new to harsher vagabond conditions. Still, I recognized the marks of cruelty inflicted by the strong on the weak. Spirelight or not, my blood heated up. It was nothing compared to the fuming murder I saw in Shelov's eyes.

My brother and I made a lot of silly jokes so the girl laughed through her sobs. She said more than once, "Thanks. You guys are the best!"

Before long, a trio of dusky, strapping male shapes came lurching uphill through the deepening night. They passed the bonfire, turned towards the gathering hall, and headed our way. I kept an eye on them. The girl stepped behind Shelov.

The one in the lead still spotted her. He shouted, "That Clea? Hey, Clea, don't be like that! Why'd you run off from the party, bitch? Aw, c'mon on back, girl."

Shelov had the jug of sap-wine in hand. He took a deep pull and set it on the railing. Still calm, he walked off the porch and down towards the guys. I followed him. The girl stayed put. The guys all wore blades on their belts. I slowed up when I spotted this. Shelov didn't.

Shelov got right up in the lead guy's face. "Okay, look, boys, fun's over. I don't know what's goin' on, 'cept the lady obviously ain't in the mood for it. Best thing right now for everyone here is y'all just take it easy, steer clear, and we can all enjoy the rest of the festival, no harm, no –"

"*Lady?*" said the one to the left, a tall, gangly, hatchet-faced punk. He squinted up at the torch-lit porch. "Listen to this crazy rover talkin' all fancy. I don't see no *lady* up there. All I see's some uppity glowstick tail, bein' a tease."

"Out of the way, rover," said the leader, stocky as Shelov but taller, with fewer scars and thicker, shorter hair. "This shit ain't your business." He gave Shelov a light shove to the chest.

Shelov bobbed backwards, came back, and let his hard fist fly. It caught the leader square in the center of his face so blood squirted from both nostrils. The guy lurched back, squinting and jerking all over the place, then stumbled and sank to his knees. The guy on the right ripped his blade from its scabbard and hacked at Shelov like he was cutting weeds. Shelov stepped forward to the right, pivoted, caught the arm in both palms, and broke it in three places with one smooth motion. I winced at the echoing crack and the shrill shriek. The guy on the left – the one who'd opened his mouth first – rushed Shelov from the side, so I rushed at him. He spotted me coming, drew his blade, and pointed it at my neck. I didn't have a blade, so I just skidded to a halt and lifted my hands. Shelov had picked up the fallen blade. He calmly placed the edge against the guy's neck. It was that asshole's turn to throw up his hands, after dropping his long knife, of course. He backed away, then turned and ran back downhill, away from the bonfire, into the night, towards the center of the village. By now, all the other revelers had stopped to stare at us. Shelov snarled at them all. They all turned away and drifted back awkwardly into the motion of their revels.

Shelov hauled up both of the fallen guys, one on each arm. "Okay, fun's over, boys. I'm haulin' your asses home. Sleep it off." I made to follow. He shook his head at me. "Where you think you're goin', boy? Go make sure that girl's okay." He went off hauling those guys home.

I went back and comforted Clea. So did some of my fellow native lady-friends who'd seen it all happen. They did a better job comforting her than I did. They were the ones who wound up escorting her home that night, to the huts on the other side of the village, where the refugee Spirelights lived. Soon afterwards, everyone else forgot the disturbance and got back into the swing of the festivities.

When Shelov wandered back, some other guys cautioned him in dour tones. "Oh, now you done it, Shelov. That was Dex, the chief's son, you just done fucked up. You don't fuck with Dex's boys like that, unless you want a war."

Shelov snorted, shrugged, and chugged more sap-wine. "War? Heh. Fuck those guys, and fuck you too. That punk don't know what war is. Neither do you. Someone get me another damn drink."

Until recently, most of us born and raised in the remote mountain village of Lehirn, we'd known of Spirelights only as Imperialist assholes in the world out there. Most of us had never even seen one, just heard the stories. We learned of them from the tale-leaves, carried in by vagabonds, mostly of our own race, along with the occasional runaway slave Ghestru. Our village had always been open to shelter whatever desperate vagabonds and fugitives could find it, so long as they pulled their weight pitching in and didn't make trouble. That's how it went, for a few generations now. 'Til the coming of Magur Sevi, none of us had ever expected such destitute travelers to include Spirelights.

The Nagga mountains, it seemed, were one of the few secluded regions that remained untouched by the genocidal strife that now engulfed the lands beyond. In a thousand years, the Spirah Empire had cut just one lonely, secluded road between our lowest foothills, used only for the most clandestine northward transport. All indigenous inhabitants dwelt deeply within the treacherous, wild ranges beyond, not worth their trouble. We didn't bother them, and they didn't bother us. We'd learned not to wander too far past certain borders, past the Nagga River to the south, or the Schlogmire marshes to the west, the ocean to the east, or the frosty, crusty wastelands to the north, between the next ocean and the lands of Spiralla. Anyone with too restless a roving foot got what they asked for.

My brother Shelov had struck out far, taken what he'd found, and returned to us defiantly proud of everything the lands had made of him. There were fighters among us, sure. Sometimes we feuded with neighboring mountain tribes. My brother was something else. While he wandered, troops from the nearby Spirelight city-state of Trescha took him prisoner, forced him to fight for their amusement in their low-tier combat pits, recognized his skill and ferocity, then enlisted him into their international wars of conquest. He'd earned some renown. Once he got sick of it, he murdered his commanding officer in the night and decided it was time to come home to the Nagga Mountains. Whatever he went through out there, he never liked to talk about it much. He told me more than most.

In recent years, though, things have changed out there, in the world beyond these mountains. After all these centuries, it's finally pushing itself inward, into our hills...just not like we expected. Travelers talk of a race of humanoid monsters called the Crimbone...*the beast-race.* People say the Crimbone evolved from us, the Schomites. The Crimbone wield black blades, forged of an unbreakable, otherworldly metal. No one knows where this metal comes from, or how they forge their weapons from it. They say the black metal drinks the living essence of the Spirelights they kill, the divine essence of the tyrannical gods of the Spirah pantheon within all Spirelights. Every time a Crimbone drinks the dying glow of a Spirelight's divine essence, that Crimbone grows more powerful and harder to kill. No one's figured out what causes someone to be an ordinary Schomite one day, a Crimbone called off to blood-thirsty feasting the next. No Crimbone have turned up in our village. Every day, more of us grow scared and paranoid that one will.

They've been around out there for a while, these Crimbone, well before my parents were born, a scattered aberration. In the last few years, though, people say a new chief has risen among them, uniting them...the one they call Magur Sevi, the Blazing Chief. They say he flies from land to land, on the back of a great dragon. He's sworn to burn the world the Spirah Empire has made to the ground, so something can grow anew from the lands. Since the rise of Magur Sevi, displaced civilian Spirelights have flooded into the Nagga mountains, scraggly and desperate, nothing like I was led to picture them. The local chiefs – our wise men and wise women – have welcomed them, urged us to tolerate them as fellow desperate creatures of our lands. Some of us have accepted them. Others haven't. Many Spirelights cling priggishly to the snooty manners of their fallen glory, out among all us hill-tribe ruffians. They haven't done themselves any favors with that, them or their fellows who'd rather make peace within whatever secluded safe-haven will take them.

A few weeks later, my brother and I got up early, ventured deep into the woods for some hunting, and tracked our way down alongside the river, as we often did. I brought along my sling and a pouch full of sharp, jagged throwing-chunks. So did Shelov. He also brought his blade, a blue-shimmering two-foot sliver of water-monster-scale, the hardest, sharpest material anyone up here had ever seen. Ever since the night of the festival, he never went anywhere without it. Sometimes I caught up with Clea. I didn't like having to venture into the Spirelight hut-town to find her, but I made myself do it. The Spirelights there all side-eyed me, but none of them attacked. The chief's son hadn't bothered her since, she claimed, and neither had the rest of his boys, but she rarely ventured from the Spirelight hut-town anymore. Now and then, though, I caught menacing glances from the friends of the guys my brother had fucked up. If he noticed, he never mentioned it.

As we tracked our way downriver, I said, "I still don't get why you have so much sympathy for all these glowsticks, man. I mean, from what you've told me...y'know, of what you went through out there...they all sound like a bunch of asshole monsters."

Shelov didn't answer at first. Then he sat on a rock, drew his blade, set to polishing and sharpening it. "Yeah?

So how 'bout all these glowsticks livin' with us lately? They seem so monstrous to you, boy?"

Like I mentioned, I was older than Shelov, by a few years. Since he'd come home, though, he'd taken to calling me *boy*. It still pissed me off, but I didn't feel like stoking his temper, so I just said, "I guess not."

"There you go, then." He kept sharpening his blade. "Anyway, most Spirelights I met out there, yeah, they were monsters to me, sure enough. They're humanoid, after all, so your description ain't wrong. These ones livin' with us lately, though...well, I see how a lot of our own treat 'em, like the chief's son and his pack of morons. It ain't so different from how I was treated out there, by Spirelights, back when they ruled the world, before this Magur Sevi asshole, whatever the fuck he is, started rilin' up all these Crimbone bastards to turn the world into an even bigger pile of shit."

Something whistled through the air. A crunch echoed next to me. Shelov lurched and hiccuped. I spun towards him. He spilled forward and splashed into the water. At first, half of him lay face down in the flow, his back half stretched across the sandy bank. Then the current caught him and pulled him off. He floated downhill, bumping off the juts of rocks like a stray clump of fallen leaves. His sword landed in the water next to him and sank. I shouted at him, but got no answer. I spun and looked uphill, just in time to see a fleeing shape I recognized vanish over yonder hillside...the kind wearing the colors of the chief's son and his pals. I darted downhill after Shelov, even though I already knew he was dead. By the time I caught up with his body, there was no point in hoping. He'd lodged himself against a jut of rock, right in front of a little waterfall. His arms and legs dangled and rippled forward limply, his blood and brains pulsing out of his shattered skull, into the downhill flow.

I found his blade where it had settled, uphill from where he had. I wiped the water from it and stalked back uphill, looking for his killers. I scoured the surrounding trails and gullies all day. I couldn't find them. They were long gone. It ain't the style of such cowards to stick around, once they've done their dirty work from out of harm's way. I ran back to town and brought back the local magistrate. The authorities said it looked like some of the vagabond Spirelight rabble had done it. I drew my own conclusions. Over the next week, the magistrate's men and women had an excuse to beat up a lot of Spirelight refugees.

Here's what I ain't told you yet, though, about my brother, or about me. After he came home, he took it upon himself to put me through hell. He whipped me into shape, forced me to learn how to wield a sword properly, how to sneak around in the woods, how to be a hunter...how to be a murderer, the kind who gets up close and does his work face to face. There were hunters among us, and fighters, but few real warriors. I didn't think I'd ever have to use what my brother forced me to learn, outside of friendly sparring. But he made sure I learned. Oh, yeah, buddy, believe it, I learned. I kept that scale-blade of his, too, and I made sure it stayed polished and sharp.

I was off my guard, off that game, on that night when it started, when the chief's son and his pals tried to rape that Spirelight girl, and my brother stopped it. I was also off my game on the day my brother died, since I watched him sink into the river. Ever since, I've stayed sober, on my game. I wasn't the only one of of our pals who he'd whipped into shape. I got together with the rest, whenever I could, fought them all hard, kept us all in shape, got myself sharp as I could. I never mentioned why. Between the lot of us, it was all just friendly sportsmanship.

Since getting myself in the best possible fighting shape, I spent a lot of time out in the woods around the village, stalking through the trees quietly, listening to people talk, Schomites and Spirelights alike. I waited patiently. I made sure I was stalking the right assholes. Lehirn's a small village. It wasn't hard. Schomite chiefs aren't the men or women they used to be, even here. Nor did it take long for Dex and his boys to get drunk enough and start bragging about what they'd done. Surprise, surprise, our local peace-keepers ain't done shit about it.

My late brother's blade of choice was the best, sharpest metal around, if you're not a Crimbone with wherever their infernal black metal comes from. Hell, fuck the Crimbone. They call themselves the beast race? They say they evolved from us Schomites? I've got a Schomite beast to show 'em, right here, motherfucker.

Once I was ready, I gave it a few weeks. After that, I went hunting by night. I thought of my brother, how all the young braves of our village wanted him to lead the Howling Hunt on the night of the festival. Most elsewhere in the world, we hear, the Spirelights have outlawed the Howling Hunt. It's a full-moon midnight rampage through the woods, where young Schomite would-be warrior boys and girls reenact the slaughter of the Old Gods, celebrating the dominion of the lands over outer celestial forces, such as those the Spirelights follow. I didn't howl, and I wasn't out to enforce anyone's dominion over anyone else. I just wanted revenge.

I took all the smaller, hard-to-spot trails Shelov had shown me throughout the hills, all the way to the little camp-out spot where the chief's son and his boys liked to have their nighttime revels. I watched them silently from the brush, 'til I spotted Gorm, the one who'd put a blade to my throat while I was unarmed, while Shelov beat up Dex for trying to rape Clea. I watched him wander out alone, into the bushes to take a piss. He wore the same blade on his belt that he'd pulled on me. He'd dropped it when Shelov checked him, but he'd retrieved it since. I circled him closer and closer, through the shadowy bushes. He finished pissing and put his junk away. I waited for him to turn around, see me there with my glimmering blade ready, just so he'd have time for it to sink in who I was, why I was there to kill him.

He squinted hard. His eyes adjusted in the gloom, and I saw that he recognized me, knew the business between us. His blade sang free with a singing hiss. He flew at me with a howl, chopping wildly. I stepped in to meet him with an upward block. Our blades clashed and locked. While he pressed down strong, I stepped past him, let my blade role out and around from beneath his. He careened forward, off balance. I stepped through, pivoted, let my edge sail down in a clean whistle, and sliced his head from his shoulders. The rest of him fell and slid through the grass next to me. Blood coughed from his neck across the grass. I'd caught him by the hair, so his severed head now dangled from my other fist by the hair. I lifted it skyward.

There's nothing like it, I tell you, that first time you kill another man in combat...that time-freezing rush, when you realize you won by a hair, how you're still alive and he's dead. The rest sets in much later, when you have time to think about how you've taken someone's life. If you don't know what I'm talking about, good for you.

The problem at the moment was, Gorm got out a scream before I took his head. My vision cleared from the rush, and I spotted the lighted doorway of the shack from which he'd come. Some of his pals came out, stumbling over each other, including Dex and that other asshole he'd had with him on the night of the festival. I still stood far enough out in the shadows that I could have dashed back into the trees without any of them ever having a clue who I was. I was on fire, though. I felt crazy, and I loved it. I lifted Gorm's head high in my fist, waving it around for all of them to see. They all shouted and rushed me at once. I chucked the head sailing through the air, so it hit the first of them, square in the noggin. He kept rushing forward and skewered himself on my point. When I jerked the blade out of him, his whole belly slit open, so his guts spilled and bubbled noxiously over my hand. The stench almost made me vomit. I choked it back, because the others swarmed in past him, shouting, all over me, brandishing blades of their own...not real war-blades, just whatever sharp chunks of metal they had lying around.

None of them were skilled. They outnumbered me eight to one, though, and they were pissed, and most of them were bigger than me. My brother would have made short work of them all and called it a fair fight. I'm not my brother. Still, I ducked, and wove, and bobbed through them, hacking, blocking and evading as I went. I got stabbed in the shoulder, in the side, in the ass. Their blood and guts splashed all over me, stinging my open wounds, so I couldn't help wondering where those bastards had been. Once I realized I'd killed them all, fatigue set in so I figured I'd fall over and die any second. That didn't happen, so I staggered off into the woods. Once I was far off enough to figure I was safe, I sat down and tended to my wounds. Infection set in, but I still didn't dare go back to the village, even though I already knew there was no way my crime had been discovered yet.

As I hid out in the woods, I kept expecting to hear boots thundering towards me, after discovering what I'd done. They never came. Since then, I've become a wanted man, among my own people. It's been years now, though really not so long a time.

My fever got worse, and I grew delirious. I staggered around in the woods, through a fevered days. Eventually, I wandered close enough towards civilization that someone caught me, guided me home to their hut, and nursed me back to health. They also made sure the village authorities never found out they were sheltering me there. It turned out, it was Clea who found me and saved my ass. For a while, I dwelt in the Spirelight refugee hut-town. Once I was back on my feet, I took to the woods again and lived out there. My brother had taught me how. Clea and her people kept coming to see me. They kept me posted on what was going on.

More Spirelight refugees filtered in, as shit got worse and worse out in the rest of Deschemb. People now say that this Magur Sevi is something other than a Crimbone. No one knows what the hell he is. Some swear he's a demon of vengeance, set loose by the lands themselves, to punish us all. These days, even this far up in the hills, we can smell the burning-meat stench of the carnage he leaves in his wake, as the dragon he rides breaths out fire and his Crimbone braves charge forth through it. They say Magur

Sevi and his dragons are coming for all of us. They say he's heard of Spirelights and Schomites striking peaceful alliances, and he hates that worse than anything. Magur Sevi's forces are pushing into these hills, like the Spirah empire never had the guts to do.

Meanwhile, I spend my nights with Clea. We're pretty much husband and wife now. Yeah, I know what I said earlier, about Spirelight girls. Times were different then, though, and so was I. As to her people, I've readied them for battle as best I can. One by one, I've taught them the ways of the sword, beaten them into shape for war, like my brother taught me. The best of my students have passed it on to their brothers and sisters.

Within days, from what our scouts tell us, the forces of Magur Sevi will be here upon us. The smoke smells closer. I breath it in deeply, eager to meet whatever end it brings. Soon, the outside world will come to kill us. I'll lead my people to face it on our feet. We'll die as one, together. Bring it on, bitches. I'll meet you down by the river.

Story Notes

The Room Above The Bar On River Street: Sturgeon, Vermont is a fictional place that my stories sometimes find their way to. It's an amalgamation of memories and experiences from my drifter days, in many rural towns I stayed in or passed through at some point. Pretty much everyone and everything painted in this story is real, or once was, or seemed to be at the time. The supernatural element is just my wacky imagination...or is it? Nah, just kidding...or am I?

Kids Say The Weirdest Things: This happened spontaneously, in a morbidly cheeky frame of mind, while I was living out in Guilford, Vermont with my fiancée at the time. One day I got home from work, and she told me how the neighbor's kid had wandered over to hang out with her while she was working in the garden. The kid started babbling at her about life, like little kids do. He talked about how he and his family had gone to church that day. Apparently, there'd been some kind of holiday ceremony, in which he'd been invited to take part. Somewhere in there, he said something like, "And then the Priest poured blood on my head." I'm pretty sure it wasn't real blood, but who the fuck knows, right? When my fiancée told me about it, I got to ruminating about having been raised Catholic, and on how weird and toxic organized religion can be. So I typed out the anecdote more or less as she'd told it to me, and embellished it into something outright grotesque and otherworldly.

No One Rides For Free: Even all these years after my teenage Goth-boy phase, I'm still a sucker for a good vampire story. Vampires, when done right, are endlessly versatile mythological creatures, fodder for great yarns, as both protagonists and antagonists. There have been whole books written on the subject of why they continue to resonate in our collective consciousness. If you're interested in the subject, I recommend the book *Our Vampires, Ourselves* by Nina Auerbach. The vampires in this story owe a lot to Lonesome Cowboy Bill's Hot Rod Vampires, a creation for an episode on which we collaborated for his late-night radio program *Moby's Trip* on KKFI, Kansas City Community Radio. A very different version of this tale first materialized in a novel that died on me, but had a few choice scenes, with some strong imagery and characterization, which I decided were worth cannibalizing into stand-alone short-stories. What fascinated me here is the idea of vampires as just one more kind of sketchy folks you might encounter while roaming the country...how to someone *in the know*, so to speak, awareness of their existence isn't even a big deal. Like many folks you meet out there, they're a dangerous lot, who play by their own rules, and you're wise not to let your guard down around them. If you know how to not set a foot wrong, though – and if you have the stomach for it – they can be fun to chill with for a while. In fact, a pack of supernatural blood-suckers might not be so bad, compared to the kind of scumbaggery all us plain ol' humans are capable of inflicting upon each other.

Have Some Dragon's Blood: This story happened because I found I loved the scent of Dragon's Blood incense, so I did a little historical research, which marinated in my brain with all sorts of world mythology I'd been reading about dragons lately. I started thinking about the discrepancy between Christian and pre-Christian myths about dragons, particularly Saint George and related stories. From there, I started typing and this happened.

Paulie, Ronnie, and Michelle: Michelle's reminiscences are based on a mix of fact, fiction, unreliable memories, and everything in between. This story – and its epistolary form – happened because I listened to Neko Case's cover of Tom Waits's *Christmas Card From A Hooker In Minneapolis*, while I was in a particularly wistful frame of mind, by which I mean I was stoned off my ass. The song pulled at something in me, broke my heart in all the right places…because I'd met that narrator, in multiple incarnations in real life, including a lady I used to live with in New Orleans. I wondered what had become of her, since we'd passed like ships in the night, as the saying goes. I threw on more tunes, packed a fresh bowl, and typed the first draft of this story. The twist at the end – or more specifically, how it's presented – reflects a dangerous, oblivious selfishness that's all too common in human nature; Michelle doesn't even notice the ironic juxtaposition of informing Paulie that she's just placed him in danger and signing off with love. The town of Meredith Falls is the creation of Rebecca Croteau, a longtime friend and fellow author. If you're in the mood to read a ripping good werewolf yarn that's both sexy and scary as all fuck, with some fresh twists on old tropes, do yourself a favor and grab a copy of her novel *Clearer in the Night*. You're welcome. I used the location here, with permission, essentially as an inside joke. And yes, that weird old little antiques dealer Michelle mentions is the same one from *Have Some Dragon's Blood.*

Lambs of Slaughter in Blue and Gold: I spun this one up based on a writing prompt, for a proposed anthology of stories all inspired by the same water-color painting. The painting showed the face of a pretty, wistful-eyed young lady in the foreground, surrounded by a picturesque rural, dreamy backdrop, haunted by a cast of spectral shapes, suggesting many harrowing, bittersweet memories. Behind the girl, there arose some long-limbed, skeletal, demonic being, something threatening...or watching over her like a guardian spirit...or perhaps something in between. I still have a scan of that painting somewhere around here, but unfortunately, I can't show it to you, for copyright reasons. Plus, at the time, I'd just started a new relationship, and in that sort of whimsical romantic reverie, I kept throwing Bonnie Tyler's *Total Eclipse of the Heart* on my writing music playlist. So this story happened. The editors accepted it, then as *Oh fuck me* luck would have it, the bastards canceled it because they couldn't find enough good contributors to fill the whole anthology. I still really like this story, though.

Dead Men, Dead Dogs, Tasty Bacon: Some anthology guidelines said *Do something new with zombies*, or something to that effect. So I introduced these guys, then threw the dog at them and watched what happened. Yes, the doctor's name is a shamelessly coy Lovecraft reference. Yes, I'm pretty sure, Sean is the same guy from *The Room Above The Bar On River Street*, at an earlier time in his life.

Just Chew Your Way Out: This isn't the first story I wrote starring Cassias Morningstar, and I didn't realize when I started it that it was an "origin story" of sorts. Cassias is usually funnier than this, not so angry and depressing. His exploits are typically closer to snarky, affectionate parody of Sword & Sorcery fantasy (a genre I unabashedly love, in case you hadn't noticed). I wrote this during the aftermath of a rather bleak, traumatic time in my life. I still don't like to talk about it to most people. The story came out while I was still processing all the anger, confusion, feelings of betrayal and resentment (some accurate, others misguided in hindsight), sorting out what I'd lost, what I'd learned, how I'd changed...hopefully for the better, but I wasn't there yet, not even close. Relax, folks, I didn't actually go on a killing spree. Here's the thing about turbulent experiences that irrevocably change us, for better and/or worse: we, as humans, typically don't remember them as they actually happened, so much as how they *felt*. This makes writing larger-than-life otherworldly fantasy a uniquely perfect cathartic outlet for such raw emotions. At least it is for me. Along the way, I got the chance to subvert a few classical fairy tale/mythological tropes, like the sleeping princess.

Useful Instincts: This Sean Harris yarn was originally published in the sadly now-defunct crime fiction magazine

STORY TIME WITH CRAZY UNCLE MATT

Hard Luck Stories. It began as a free-writing exercise, and became one of my earliest professional sales, and I felt very proud. Partially due to the guideline/genre constraints, it foregoes my usual supernatural flourishes...or does it? I left that aspect intentionally ambiguous, so decide for yourself.

Island of Skulls: I wrote this one as a two-part serial for the first two issues of *Broadswords and Blasters*, a fine retro-pulp magazine run by Matthew Gomez and Cameron Mount, still going strong as of this writing. Tia and Ketz first showed up as supporting players in my novel *Changing of the Guards* (forthcoming from Azure Spider publications). They stuck in the back of my mind as characters it might be fun to write about as the main protagonists. Then Gomez asked me to write something for his new magazine, and this is what I came up with. It turned out to be a *lot* of fun, and I've written a good deal more about these protagonists since. The history of the lands of Deschemb is referenced throughout my urban fantasy novels *The Night and the Land* and *The Trail of the Beast*. Due to the weirdness of the publishing industry, this became the first tale to see print actually set in Old Deschemb, where I got to drop the reader into the middle of it with the characters, sink or swim, which to my taste, is the best way to handle one's personal mythological landscape in fiction.

The Reverend: I invented the character of the Reverend as a secondary persona, back when I was a radio DJ. I've always loved the dark-Americana iconography of the black-clad fire-an'-brimstone ol' timy traveling preacher, despite my general real-life suspicion and disdain for organized religion. This ominous, unapologetically romanticized persona is equal parts Robert Mitchum in *The Night of the Hunter* (one of my all-time favorite films) and some ancient, ageless trickster spirit, forever weaving their way in and out of our collective experiences, taking many forms, whose true motives aren't ours to know. I can't remember what inspired the 1960s setting, but I drew it feverishly from my impressions of the era, from hazy anecdotes told to me by folks who were there, such as the narrator. For whatever I got right, thank them. For whatever I got wrong...well, I hope you still enjoy the tale. *Can I get an Amen, brothers and sisters!*

The Proper Word is Blackmail: This one began with the macabre opening imagery, along with Frederick's spontaneous use of fancy tableware. I filled out the rest of the story around it, and in the process tied up some loose ends from the one completed Hawthorne novel to date, *Cult of the Stars*. After including *Have Some Dragon's Blood* in this collection, I thought it only fitting to treat sharp-eyed readers to a little snapshot of Frederick and Inspector Hawkins in their usual element, such as it is.

Nagga Mountain Blues: This one goes out to the memory of the late great Mike Dabney. In case anyone wonders, yes, that's the same mountain village Tia and Ketz come from, but at least six hundred years after their lifetime. It was a chance to put a humanized face on the background folks in events referenced in *The Night and the Land*. Folks have written me with raw reactions to this story, equating it with this or that thing about modern times. Like everything else about Deschemb, I drew on history, mythology, my imagination, alt-country music stuck in my head at the time, and some of my own experiences cranked up to eleven. What you make of it from there is your own business. It feels like a fitting way to close out this collection.

Matt Spencer is the author of the novels *The Night and the Land*, *The Trail of the Beast*, *Summer Reaping on the Fields of Nowhere*, *Cult of the Stars* (illustrated by Deirdre Burke) and *The Drifting Soul* (illustrated by Stephen R. Bissette), as well as numerous novellas and short stories. He's been a journalist, New Orleans restaurant cook, factory worker, radio DJ, and a no-good ramblin' bum. He's also a song lyricist, playwright, actor, and martial artist. As of this writing, he lives in Brattleboro, Vermont.

Thanks for reading, everybody! Hope you enjoyed the ride. Be a pal and don't forget to go online to Amazon, Goodreads, whatever social media you're into, and drop a short review (or a long one if you feel like it).

9 780692 156384